FINDING GOD
IN THE
MOUNTAINS
OF
AFGHANISTAN

Joshua Pennifield

Dedication

I would like to dedicate this book to:

To all my fellow servicemen and women out there who paid the ultimate price.

Table of Contents

Preface

The desert sun had barely crested the skyline at Fort Bliss, Texas, but Staff Sergeant Michael "Stache" Anderson was already wide awake. It wasn't just the heat, or the schedule—they were used to that. It was something deeper. This deployment felt different. Sharper. Like God was going to do more than just send them overseas—He was going to do something inside them.

The days leading up to their departure were filled with the kind of grind that tests men—SRP lines, CLS certifications, weapons qual, and endless convoy drills across unforgiving terrain. Stache led his squad through every station, every task, knowing the stakes. Every test passed; every course completed brought them closer to the mountains of Afghanistan. And every night brought Stache a little deeper into a quiet wrestling with his own soul.

Raised on Scripture but hardened by service, Stache had drifted far from his faith. Still, somewhere in the noise of training and duty, there was a whisper—a stirring he couldn't shake. Men like Specialist Dave Wilson spoke often about Scripture and led the squad in prayer. Others like Foster were skeptical, carrying scars and silence. It was in that tension—between belief and battle—that Stache found himself searching again.

The Bible his mother had given him—tucked in the side pocket of his rucksack—had been gathering dust. But the night before wheels-up, under the vast Texas sky, Stache pulled it out. Psalm 23:4 caught his eye: "Even though I walk through the valley of the shadow of death, I will fear no evil, for you are with me." And for the first time in a long while, he let the Word speak to him.

This book isn't just a story about war.

It's a story about finding God in the middle of it.

These chapters follow Stache and his squad—not just through firefights and convoys, but through doubt, prayer, laughter, loss, and ultimately, transformation. You'll meet a group of men who, despite differences in belief and background, became a brotherhood forged in fire.

And between the lines of camo and chaos, you'll see the hand of a faithful God calling one soldier back home—to Himself.

If you've ever felt distant from God… if you've struggled to reconcile faith with real-world pain… or if you just need a reminder that grace still finds us in the most unlikely places—this story is for you.

Welcome to *Finding God in the Mountains of Afghanistan.*

Chapter 1: PMCS and the Weight of Command

The sun clawed its way over the cracked desert floor of Fort Bliss, casting sharp rays across a motor pool full of half-awake soldiers and dust-caked Humvees. The kind of light that didn't warm you—just exposed everything it touched. Staff Sergeant Michael "Stache" Anderson stood next to his truck, arms crossed, watching his squad file in with sluggish steps and bloodshot eyes. He'd already been up for hours.

"Move like you got purpose," he barked. Not a shout, but with enough gravel in his voice to get heads turning.

The morning had already tasted like burnt coffee and diesel fumes. It was a Fort Bliss kind of morning—dry, loud, relentless. Stache had been through this routine more times than he could count, but this deployment felt different. Not in a dramatic, gut-feeling sort of way. Just heavier. Like every checklist item carried more consequence.

He glanced down at the day's training schedule. Another block of PMCS. Preventive Maintenance Checks and Services. Boring to most. But it saved lives. Or cost them.

He called his squad to formation.

"Alright, listen up. We roll out in three weeks. These trucks? They go with us. If one breaks down in the middle of a convoy in the Korangal, it's not just inconvenient—it's a target painted on our backs. Today, we PMCS by the book. Fluids, belts, tires, electronics, comms, armor plates. Nothing gets skipped. If you miss a fault, you're not screwing over a motor sergeant. You're screwing over your brothers."

The squad murmured affirmatives. Some more awake than others.

He walked the line.

Specialist Perez, new to the unit, gave a sharp nod, trying too hard. Private Kyle "KJ" Johnson already had grease on his hands, half-listening while eyeing the hood of an MRAP. Johnny Thompson, sniper, was calm, eyes already sweeping the lot like he was watching for movement, not oil leaks. And Doc— Specialist Matthews—stood quietly at the rear, checking his med kit. Always prepping. Even during PMCS.

Stache motioned toward the row of trucks.

"Get to it. I'll be coming around. Don't make me find what you should've."

The squad split off.

Twenty minutes in, the sun was already cooking the pavement. Stache moved from truck to truck, scanning clipboards, asking quiet questions, pulling dipsticks himself. He didn't micromanage—he verified.

He was halfway through checking on KJ's vehicle when Perez waved him over.

"Sergeant, truck three is done. All green."

Stache raised an eyebrow. "All green, huh?"

Perez nodded; clipboard hugged to his chest.

Stache walked over. The Humvee looked fine at a glance. But when he reached the front left side, he stopped cold. The tire was flat. Not low. Not underinflated. Flat.

He turned slowly. "Perez!"

The Specialist jogged over; the smile already gone from his face.

"You call this green?"

Perez blinked, mouth opening, closing. "I must've—must've missed it."

"You missed the tire? The part of the truck that touches the ground?"

The squad went quiet. Tools paused mid-turn. Conversations cut short. Stache stepped closer, not yelling, but low and dangerous.

"You go into a hot zone with a tire like this, you don't just break down. You die. Or someone else does while trying to cover you."

Perez swallowed.

"We're starting over," Stache said loud enough for everyone. "Everyone. Get your TMs out. You follow every step. I want a 5988-E filled out per vehicle. I don't care if you've done this a hundred times. Today you do it like it's the first."

No one groaned. That was something. But the tension in the air was thick.

Stache watched them work. Checked every fault noted. Pointed out things even the manual didn't always mention. Tension rods. Fire extinguishers out of date. Comm wire frayed. They caught most of it themselves this time.

An hour passed. Then two. The sun rose higher. Sweat soaked through uniforms. Oil stained every pair of gloves. But by noon, every 5988-E was properly filled out and reviewed.

He gathered them back in.

"You think I like riding you about this stuff? I don't. But I like writing letters to families even less. So from now on, assume your mistake could get someone killed. Because it can."

He paused. His eyes fell on Perez.

"Perez, you're riding shotgun with me for the next week. You and I are going to become best friends with every bolt on these trucks."

Perez nodded, shame on his face, but also something else. Resolve.

That evening, Stache sat alone behind the maintenance bay. The sky was soft now, bleeding orange and lavender behind the mountains. He pulled a small, worn Bible from his cargo pocket. The one his mother had given him before his first tour.

He opened to Psalm 23.

"Even though I walk through the valley of the shadow of death..."

The words rested heavy, not dramatic. Just true.

He closed the Bible and looked up. Somewhere out there, beyond this base and the desert and the drills, was a valley in Afghanistan. He didn't know what waited there. But he knew who he had to be when they got there.

And he wasn't about to let a flat tire be what brought them down.

Chapter 2: Into the Valley

Three weeks passed in a blur of checklists, weapons quals, first aid drills, and late-night reflections under the blistering Texas stars. When the day finally came, the tarmac at Biggs Army Airfield was lit in a strange half-light, the sun still hiding behind the Franklin Mountains. C-17s waited like steel monsters, their bellies open to swallow the nervous energy of a hundred troops.

Staff Sergeant Michael "Stache" Anderson shifted the weight of his rucksack, scanning the lines of soldiers boarding one by one. He spotted Johnny Thompson checking his rifle for the third time that hour, Doc kneeling near a medic's bag, reorganizing gauze and syringes by muscle memory, and Perez standing awkwardly with his kit, still too green but no longer clueless.

"Let's go, 2nd Squad," Stache called, motioning his men forward.

Inside the aircraft, the air was thick with diesel fumes and anticipation. The deafening roar of engines drowned out conversation, which was fine by most. Some soldiers stared blankly. Others gripped rosaries or flicked through photos on their phones. Stache sat near the middle, sandwiched between Perez and Jimmy Carter. Jimmy passed him a stick of gum without a word.

"You think any of us are really ready?" Jimmy asked finally, voice raised over the engines.

"No," Stache said, chewing slowly. "But we're trained. There's a difference."

The engines screamed louder, the plane shaking as it pulled from the hangar and accelerated down the runway. Boots pressed into the floor; palms gripped seat webbing. Then—lift. Everything fell silent inside Stache's head for a moment.

As the ground dropped away, he looked back down the aisle at his squad. KJ had his eyes shut tight, lips moving in silent prayer. Johnny stared out into nothing; a rifle strapped across his knees. And Doc, always calm, leaned back with his arms folded and a meditative stillness that felt both reassuring and surreal.

The flight dragged. Ten hours to Germany. Another eight to Bagram. Midway through the second leg, Jimmy tapped Stache on the shoulder and handed him a folded note.

"For when you need it," Jimmy said, then returned to staring at the aircraft wall.

Stache opened it: Psalm 46:1. God is our refuge and strength, a very present help in trouble.

He folded it back without a word, placing it carefully into his Bible. He hadn't opened the Good Book much lately, but Jimmy never pushed it. He just showed up—with verses instead of sermons.

By the time they landed in Bagram, the sun was blinding and the air thinner. The mountains loomed like teeth around the airfield, jagged and cold. The base buzzed with movement: Black Hawks circling, trucks hauling crates, soldiers moving with precision that only came from muscle memory born of repetition and necessity.

There was no ceremony, no speeches. Just names barked, gear dumped, and instructions yelled in thick accents from soldiers already used to the madness. Stache kept his men close. Herded them through the chaos like a sheepdog guarding a flock he was determined not to lose.

A grizzled Sergeant First Class from the outgoing unit met them near the helipad.

"Korangal? You drew the short straw," he said flatly, then gestured toward a line of battered Chinooks.

Stache didn't answer. Just gave a nod and motioned for his men to board. The ride from Bagram to the Korangal Outpost would be the final stretch—and the real test.

The Chinook thundered low over jagged cliffs and narrow valleys. Below them, ancient paths snaked through dusty villages, and goat trails curled along ridges where eyes watched from behind veils and stones. Stache pressed his helmet tighter as the aircraft bucked against a pocket of turbulence.

"Feels like flying into Mordor," KJ muttered, barely audible over the roar.

"Worse," Johnny replied. "Mordor's fictional."

The ramp dropped hard at the Korangal Forward Operating Base. The valley opened before them like a wound carved into the earth. Steep slopes closed in on all sides, dotted with scraggly trees and rocks the size of cars. Stache jumped off first, boots hitting packed dirt, eyes scanning instinctively.

The base wasn't much. A collection of hesco barriers, plywood huts, and camo netting. Burn pits smoldered at the edge. Sandbags stacked like fortresses around every wall. Stache smelled burnt plastic, old sweat, and the sharp sting of dust.

A wiry lieutenant with sunburnt cheeks met them. First Lieutenant Brooks.

"Welcome to the Korangal. You're going to hate it here," he said. "But you'll survive. Maybe."

Brooks led them through the outpost, pointing out critical areas: command tent, aid station, ammo point, latrines. The men moved like ghosts, silently absorbing everything.

As they neared the motor pool, Brooks paused. "You won't be doing much driving. Roads are mostly footpaths and goat trails. But you'll want to keep the trucks running. Just in case."

Stache nodded. "We've done the PMCS. We'll keep up with it."

Brooks gave him a long look, then smirked. "Good. You're already ahead of most units that come through here."

The handoff wasn't immediate. They'd shadow the current squad for the next few weeks, learning routes, rapport with the villagers, enemy patterns. But the message was clear: this place didn't wait for anyone to feel ready.

That night, Stache lay in his cot, the walls of his tent shaking faintly with each passing helicopter. His body was exhausted, but his mind raced.

From somewhere outside, distant gunfire popped. Not close. Not alarming. Just a reminder.

He reached for his Bible, flipping to Psalm 46.

"God is our refuge and strength..."

The words didn't feel distant. Not here. Not now.

He looked at the tent roof and whispered a quiet promise:

"I will bring them home. Or die trying."

Sleep came slowly.

The Korangal waited.

Chapter 3: Baptism by Fire

First light slithered across the jagged peaks of the Korangal Valley, bathing the outpost in a muted gray-blue. Staff Sergeant Michael "Stache" Anderson was already geared up, helmet strapped, rifle slung, boots laced tight. He stood near the sandbag wall overlooking the northern ridge, sipping burnt coffee from a dented tin mug.

The morning wasn't quiet. Quiet was a myth here. The mountains groaned with wind, the occasional crack of small arms fire in the distance reminded them that peace was a temporary lie. It had been a week since their boots first hit Afghan dirt, and they were already in sync with the rhythm of the Korangal: sweat, tension, adrenaline, exhaustion. Repeat.

Jimmy approached from the barracks, yawning, cradling his own mug.

"You sleep?"

Stache shook his head. "Didn't try."

Jimmy looked out toward the horizon. "We've got the patrol with Brooks' team today. He wants us to take point—shadow the route, mark terrain."

Stache nodded, already expecting it. Their squad had trained for months, but this was the proving ground. A shadow patrol wasn't just a tour. It was a test. The Korangal didn't care how many drills you passed in Texas.

By 0600, the squad was geared up. Weapons checked, radios tested, plates adjusted. Doc moved through the team with quiet efficiency, tapping shoulders and checking IFAKs. Johnny locked eyes with Stache and gave a tight nod. KJ adjusted the strap on his ruck and muttered something about bad omens and horror movies.

Perez triple-checked his magazines, fidgeting until Stache clapped him on the shoulder. "Breathe. This ain't a test. It's your life."

They formed up behind Brooks' squad, who led them out the wire with a practiced pace. The sun was fully up now, beating down against their helmets, casting long shadows across the rocky terrain. The trail wound along a narrow ledge with a sheer drop to their left and scrub brush clinging to the slopes.

Stache kept his eyes moving. Everything here had weight. Every rock was a potential concealment. Every rise a possible ambush point. His headset buzzed.

"Movement ahead, two clicks. Could be nothing," Brooks' voice crackled.

"Roger. Holding pattern?"

"Negative. Keep moving. Eyes sharp."

An hour into the patrol, the squad rounded a bend and came to a sudden stop. A line of villagers approached from the opposite direction—men, women, children, all moving in a loose group with donkeys and bundles strapped to their backs.

Brooks raised his fist. Halt.

Stache motioned his men into a staggered line and watched. Zahir, the interpreter, stepped forward with Brooks, exchanging greetings in Pashto.

Something in the villager's tone made Stache's skin crawl. He couldn't place it. A stiffness. A glance back over the ridge.

Then Zahir turned, eyes wide. "We need to move. Now. They said Taliban passed through here last night. They're close."

Brooks turned to Stache. "Take your squad. Flank right. Secure that high point overlooking the pass. We'll cover the rear."

"Got it."

They moved fast, climbing the slope to the east. Dust filled Stache's lungs. KJ slipped once, caught by Jimmy. Perez was breathing hard but kept pace.

They reached the ridgeline just in time to see shadows moving in the trees below.

"Contacts," Johnny said, voice low. "Fifteen. Maybe more. Looks like they're trying to box us in."

Stache keyed his mic. "This is Red Two. We have eyes on enemy movement—northwest treeline. At least a squad. Setting up overwatch."

"Copy, Red Two. Hold position. Engage if they get close."

They didn't have to wait long.

Gunfire erupted from below. Muffled pops turned into a roar. Echoes bounced through the valley. Bullets kicked up dust near Stache's boots.

"Return fire!" he yelled.

Johnny took two down in quick succession. Jimmy laid suppression with his M249. Doc dragged Perez behind a boulder after a round cracked too close for comfort.

Stache fired in bursts, controlled and calm. But his heart thundered.

Then came the scream.

"KJ's hit!" Ry shouted.

Stache crawled over. KJ was clutching his thigh, blood pooling fast. Doc was already there, tourniquet out, hands moving like lightning.

"Through and through," Doc muttered. "He's stable, but we need a bird."

Stache keyed his mic again. "This is Red Two, initiating 9-line medevac request."

He started broadcasting, voice clear and fast:

"Line 1: Grid coordinates—Whiskey Bravo 2847 3912.

Line 2: Red Two, secure frequency 36.95.

Line 3: One urgent.

Line 4: None.

Line 5: Litter—one.

...Pause for confirmation...

Line 6: Patient is stable—gunshot wound to the leg.

Line 7: None.

Line 8: U.S. Military.

Line 9: Smoke—marking with red."

Command responded: "Copy that, Red Two. Dustoff inbound, ETA twelve minutes. Secure your LZ."

Twelve minutes was a lifetime in the Korangal.

"Jimmy, Johnny, shift fire left. Doc, keep him breathing. Perez, Ry—you're with me. We clear the LZ."

They scrambled down the slope to a flat spot with loose gravel. Not ideal, but their best option. Smoke popped. Red and green.

Stache glanced up. A Black Hawk buzzed overhead, circling.

"Dustoff on final. Hold positions."

The helicopter hovered as the hoist lowered. Dust whipped through the air like a sandstorm. The squad held the perimeter, rifles scanning the trees.

KJ was lifted, limp but conscious. His thumbs-up from the stretcher was shaky, but it was enough.

The bird rose, banking hard, disappearing into the haze.

Silence.

Stache exhaled for the first time in what felt like an hour.

They made it back to the outpost by sundown, dragging their boots through the dirt.

"Debrief in twenty," Brooks said. "And Stache— good call on that flank."

Stache didn't answer. Just nodded.

Back in the barracks, he sat on his cot and pulled off his helmet. Sweat-soaked, dust-caked, heartbeat still somewhere in his throat.

He reached for his Bible again.

This time, he opened it to Psalm 91:

He will cover you with his feathers, and under his wings you will find refuge...

Stache didn't read it out loud. Just let the words anchor him.

KJ was still alive. They all were.

But the valley had introduced itself.

And it did not believe in second chances.

Chapter 4: First Convoy Contact

The Korangal Valley didn't rest. It pulsed. Like a living thing.

At 0430, darkness still hung thick over the outpost, broken only by the red glow of headlamps and the occasional muttered curse as boots stomped over gravel. Staff Sergeant Michael "Stache" Anderson stood in front of a convoy manifest clipboard under a flickering light inside the staging tent, scanning route overlays and radio call signs. Today, they were the lifeline.

They'd be moving fuel and munitions to FOB Restore, deep along a winding mountain route with hairpin turns and a bad reputation.

"Alright, bring it in," Stache said, voice calm but clipped.

His squad circled up, rifles slung, body armor on, helmets in hand. Nearby, diesel engines idled in the dark.

"As Convoy Commander today, I'm giving the brief. Our route is Route Iceback, total distance 54 klicks. Primary concern is narrow passes, possible IED indicators along markers 18 through 26. Rat truck will be two minutes ahead. If we take small arms fire, we push through. If a truck gets disabled, the following vehicle will recover personnel and equipment. If conditions allow, we tow it. If not, we mark and roll. Gun trucks will cover our flanks—infantry team from Alpha 3-4 is riding in overwatch positions."

He paused.

"This is a tactical movement. No cowboy crap. Keep spacing, watch your intervals. Gut feeling something's off? Say it. Otherwise, we're wheels up at 0500."

They nodded. Even Perez.

By 0515, the convoy rolled out.

Four cargo trucks. Two MRAP gun trucks—one front, one rear. Rat truck up ahead, creeping along the serpentine mountain road, scanning for tripwires, fresh dirt, or anything out of place. Stache rode in truck two, behind the rat, scanning the ridgelines through the armored glass.

The sun had just begun brushing the peaks when the first crack echoed.

Then another. Then a burst.

"Small arms fire! 3 o'clock, ridge line!" came the voice over comms.

Stache keyed his mic. "Keep pushing! All trucks continue movement—don't stop. Gun truck one, suppress right side, 300 meters."

The convoy surged forward. Dust kicked up as engines roared, tires bouncing over broken rock and narrow shoulder. Rounds pinged off steel, sparking harmlessly.

"Truck three is hit! Engine light's on!" shouted Ry over the net.

Stache craned his neck as truck three stuttered, smoke trailing from under the hood.

"Truck four, peel right and recover! Get the crew out!"

Behind them, truck four came to a halt as the gun truck wheeled around to lay suppressive fire up the slope. Stache's truck kept rolling, preserving momentum, per SOP.

"Three's crew clear," Perez reported. "They're connecting tow cable."

Bullets snapped overhead like angry insects. Stache gritted his teeth. Gunfire was still peppering the rocks, but no RPGs, no heavy weapons.

"Get it out of the kill zone. Move it!"

A minute later, truck four's engine strained as it dragged the damaged vehicle behind it, bouncing and swaying.

"Convoy, consolidate at checkpoint Sierra. 2 klicks. Let's reorg."

At the rally point, the convoy stopped behind a bend in the terrain, shielded from line of sight. Doc was already treating a minor shrapnel wound on one of the crewmen from truck three—superficial. Lucky.

Stache hopped down from his cab, boots thudding in the dirt. The smell of hot oil, cordite, and dust filled the air.

"You good?" he asked Doc.

"Yeah. Just a graze."

Stache looked over the bullet-riddled hood of the downed truck. "Radiator's toast. She ain't rolling far."

"Copy that," Jimmy said. "We'll mark and request a recovery element. Could've been worse."

Stache exhaled through his nose. "Yeah. Could've been."

Hours later, after the supplies had been delivered and signatures taken at FOB Restore, the convoy turned back toward base. The return trip was uneventful. The kind that made you forget, just for a minute, where you were.

That night, back at the FOB, the squad sat quietly over paper plates of reheated chow. No one talked much.

The adrenaline had long since burned out, leaving behind something heavier. The silence of almost.

Later, in his bunk, Stache opened his Bible but didn't read. He just stared at the pages. Letting the stillness stretch.

They'd made it.

But the valley had shown its teeth.

And Stache knew—next time, they might not be so lucky.

Chapter 5: Mission Havoc

The sun barely crested the horizon when the dispatch orders came through. Another run. This one to COP Havoc—an isolated post tucked between two ridgelines east of their current FOB. Shorter trip. Riskier terrain.

Staff Sergeant Michael "Stache" Anderson leaned over the map inside the convoy staging area, tracing the mountain pass with a gloved finger.

"Route Widow. Steep grades, known choke points, and bad weather moving in. Intel says possible IED activity near switchbacks. We'll have Alpha 3-4 again for security in the guns."

Around him, his squad stood in a tight circle, the smell of coffee, diesel, and dust mingling in the cold morning air. KJ was still down recovering. Doc was off duty after the shoulder wound. Perez, Ry, Jimmy, and Johnny were geared and listening.

"Convoy will be three cargo trucks and two MRAPs. Rat truck's got a new mount on the .50—Thompson, you're lead again. Don't get cocky."

Johnny cracked a rare grin. "Wouldn't dream of it."

Stache glanced at Perez. He'd been quiet since their last run.

"You ready?"

Perez nodded, expression hard. "Yes, Sergeant."

"Good. Because this valley doesn't care."

At 0600, the safety brief was delivered—tight, rehearsed.

Stache made sure to highlight all resources available and unavailable for this run. "We have MEDEVAC on standby, grid-locked and tracking. No EOD riding with us, but they're staged at COP Havoc for contingency. QRF is on a 15-minute standby window. Aide and litter team will be within the convoy—Perez and Ry, you're designated. If anything goes sideways, we use what we've got. Don't assume help is instant." The squad moved out ten minutes later, engines growling as they crept along the gravel and rock.

Johnny's rat truck took the lead, easing around blind corners and sharp descents. The road hugged the mountain so close it felt like the cliff tried to breathe them in.

Perez manned comms in the second truck with Stache. Ry drove. Jimmy manned the third. The rear gun truck kept overwatch, the .240B scanning ridgelines.

They cleared the first 20 klicks with no contact. Then the radio popped.

"Rat truck to Convoy, we're seeing some fresh dig marks along the edge—marker 22. Might be nothing."

Stache's jaw tightened. "Pull up five meters and halt. Gun one, get eyes on it. Alpha 3-4, dismount and investigate. Don't touch anything unless EOD clears it."

A tense five minutes passed.

"Confirmed. Looks like a pressure plate rigged to a propane tank. Local build."

"Copy. Mark it and route around."

They detoured 100 meters through an old riverbed, bouncing over dried mud and half-buried rocks. The trucks held. Barely.

As they crested the final pass before COP Havoc, it hit.

A flash.

Then thunder.

The rat truck vanished in a ball of smoke and fire.

"IED! Rat truck down!" Perez shouted.

"Push forward!" Stache barked. "Truck two moving to recover!"

Smoke poured from the blast site. Johnny's truck was on its side, rear end mangled, flames licking at the undercarriage.

Gun truck two covered the flank, spraying suppressive fire toward a suspected trigger house 300 meters uphill.

Stache's truck skidded to a stop. He was out the door before it fully stopped, rifle raised.

"Perez! Ry! Get them out!"

The cab door of the rat truck flew open. Johnny stumbled out, coughing, one hand clutching his shoulder. The gunner wasn't as lucky. Still inside.

Perez clambered up the twisted frame, ignoring the heat, and unbuckled the gunner—a PFC from Alpha 3-4. Dead weight. Blood from the ears. Burned arm. But alive.

Together, they hauled him down.

Stache keyed his mic.

"Red Two, initiating 9-line medevac. Stand by."

He rattled off the transmission, steady despite the chaos:

"Line 1: Grid coordinates—2915 3920.

Line 2: Red Two, secure freq 36.95.

Line 3: Two urgent.

Line 4: None.

Line 5: Litter—two.

...Pause...

Line 6: Blast injuries. One unconscious, one with head trauma.

Line 7: None.

Line 8: U.S. Military.

Line 9: Smoke on mark—green."

"Copy Red Two. Dustoff inbound. ETA ten mikes."

"Perimeter tight. No one fires unless we're fired on," Stache ordered.

Gun truck returned short bursts to keep heads down.

The Black Hawk swooped in low, rotor wash kicking debris across the hillside. Medevac team fast-roped in, triaged, loaded, and lifted without a wasted motion.

Then it was over.

Stache stood beside the burned-out frame of the rat truck, helmet in his hand. Johnny sat nearby, arm wrapped, blank stare locked on the twisted wreck.

"He saved the whole line," Perez said quietly, nodding toward the injured gunner.

Stache nodded. "He did."

Jimmy came up with a clipboard. "We lost the truck. We'll mark it and get a tow team tomorrow."

"Copy. Mount up. Let's finish the drop."

That night, back in the hooch, Stache finally cracked.

Not loudly. Not in front of anyone.

Just him, a half-lit Bible, and a pencil sketch he found in the pocket of the gunner's vest. It was a drawing of home—a porch swing, a dog, a little girl with pigtails.

He stared at it for a long time.

Then he tucked it into Psalm 34 and shut the book.

The Lord is close to the brokenhearted and saves those who are crushed in spirit.

The valley took something that day.

And left something heavier in return.

Chapter 6: Tension and Triage

Convoy ops didn't pause for grief. The mission kept moving.

Two days after the rat truck strike, Staff Sergeant Michael "Stache" Anderson stood beside a replacement Humvee, clipboard in hand, scanning over the updated route manifest. This run would be longer—nearly 90 klicks—delivering generators, MREs, and mail to three different FOBs, one of them barely more than a reinforced outcropping halfway up a mountainside.

He could feel the weight in his shoulders. Not just the ruck. The memory.

"Alright, bring it in," he called.

The squad circled tight under a dim morning sky; breaths visible in the mountain air. Perez, Jimmy, Ry, Johnny—and a new face: Private Foster, fresh from replacement. No time for handshakes.

"We're running Route Spider. Three stops. Last leg runs parallel to a dried creek bed—perfect IED concealment. Rat truck is swapped and checked. Thompson's back on that post."

Johnny gave a quiet nod. Still bruised, but unshaken.

Stache held up the clipboard.

"Safety brief. MEDEVAC on standby. No EOD riding with us today—closest is FOB Kunar, 40 mikes out. QRF response is stretched thin, so we'll rely on internal defense if it kicks off. Aide and litter team is Ry and Foster. Perez, you're on comms with me."

He scanned their eyes.

"This ain't the same road twice. Assume every mile wants to kill you. That's how we come back alive."

The engines rolled at 0540. Five trucks. Two MRAPs. Rat truck took the lead, weaving through the mist like a ghost.

The convoy crept across mountain switchbacks and narrow valleys for hours. Each FOB they reached brought small relief—resupply checks, comm updates, handshakes from troops who hadn't seen fresh chow in weeks.

By mid-afternoon, they reached the final stretch. The road narrowed into a serpentine path that ran beside the cracked basin of an old river. Dust kicked up thick behind the wheels.

Perez's voice came over comms. "Traffic's heavy on channel three. Another unit hit a pressure plate yesterday on a route near here."

"Copy," Stache said. "Eyes open."

They kept a steady crawl—25 kph, no more.

Then the front radio crackled.

"Rat truck to Red Two. We've got what looks like a stacked rock pile left side—marker 54."

Stache keyed his mic. "Gun one, overwatch left ridge. Rat truck, halt movement. All other vehicles hold position."

Alpha 3-4 dismounted. Two infantrymen swept forward, scanning with metal detectors. One of them signaled.

"It's wired," came the report. "Looks like it's active."

"Mark it. Back route?"

"Only option is a dry gulch—tight squeeze, soft ground."

Stache ran a hand down his face.

"Alright. We roll one at a time. Gun trucks stagger. Maintain spacing and speed."

They rerouted, tires crunching over dried roots and buried debris. Truck three nearly bogged down but recovered.

Stache kept his hand on the dash the whole way.

With less than 10 klicks to the last drop, the ridge lit up.

Gunfire.

AKs and DShKs from high ground—ambush.

Stache's voice was calm. "All trucks continue movement. Push through. Gun trucks, suppress north ridge."

Rockets streaked overhead, missing wide but enough to jar the convoy into full reaction mode. Dirt exploded beside truck two.

"Truck three hit!" Ry yelled. "Front axle's shot—we're losing power."

"Truck four, recover! Get the crew out!"

Perez was already moving. Foster dismounted with him, bullets sparking around them.

"Smoke out!" someone called, popping cover to mask movement.

The two wounded from truck three were dragged clear—one with a fractured leg, the other unconscious.

Stache keyed into medevac.

"Red Two, 9-line medevac inbound."

He fired off the lines as rounds zipped overhead:

"Line 1: Grid 3124 3877

Line 2: Red Two, secure freq 36.95

Line 3: Two urgent

Line 4: None

Line 5: Litter—two

...Pause...

Line 6: GSW and suspected TBI

Line 7: None

Line 8: U.S. Military

Line 9: Orange smoke on mark."

"Dustoff en route. ETA seven mikes."

The Black Hawk didn't waste time. It tore over the hill like vengeance, flaring hard into the LZ.

Gunner suppressed. Litter team moved.

Victims loaded.

Wheels up.

The convoy reached the final FOB at dusk.

Stache climbed from his truck, face blackened with soot, heart bruised but steady.

Inside the TOC, the major on duty saluted him.

"Heard you brought 'em in hot."

Stache didn't return the smile. "Just brought them in."

That night, he sat alone in the makeshift chapel.

It was nothing more than plywood, a few folding chairs, and a wooden cross carved into a crate.

He left his helmet on the seat next to him.

The air was still. For once.

He opened his Bible—not to read, just to hold.

Sometimes, presence was enough.

Outside, the mountains watched in silence.

But tonight, they didn't bite.

Chapter 7: Mail Call and Memories

Mail had finally caught up.

The squad sat scattered inside the briefing tent, gear shed but weapons still close. Cardboard boxes and folded envelopes littered the center table. The kind of mail drop that could change a man's mood for better or worse in under five seconds.

Perez tore into his envelope like a starving man. His smile crept in slow, followed by a shaky laugh.

"Wife sent a picture of our baby girl," he said, holding up a wrinkled photo. "She's teething on my PT belt."

The squad chuckled.

Even Johnny cracked a grin.

Ry thumbed through two envelopes. One was marked RETURN TO SENDER. The other had no return address. He opened it anyway. Inside, a single sentence: I hope you're better than you used to be.

He folded it, unreadable. Tossed it in his pocket.

Stache moved through them slowly, checking in with each soldier.

"What'd you get, Jimmy?"

"Cookies," Jimmy said, mouth already half-full. "And a five-pound bag of Sour Patch Kids. My mom doesn't believe in moderation."

Foster looked stunned as Jimmy tossed candy into the air and caught it.

"Share or suffer," Jimmy warned with mock authority.

Foster held up a tightly packed box. "Mine had socks. And a letter from my old pastor. He said he prays for our squad every night."

"Good," Stache said. "We need all the prayers we can get."

Johnny held up a can of dip. "Care package from my brother. No note. Just knew I'd be running low."

Laughter echoed softly. For a moment, the war felt miles away.

After chow, the squad peeled off one by one. Some to maintenance checks. Some to bunks. Stache stayed behind, the only light now a string of red bulbs hanging low like blood moons.

He pulled his envelope from his breast pocket. The return address was smudged, but he knew the handwriting. His sister.

He opened it with military precision. Inside were three pages. The first was typed. The second handwritten. The third a sketch—a lopsided tree next to a small white house.

He read each word slowly. Something about the deliberate pace helped him hear her voice. Her writing was sharp, warm. It didn't avoid the war, but it didn't dwell on it either.

Mom still lights a candle every Sunday, she wrote. Dad pretends he doesn't notice, but I saw him carry your picture out to the shed last week. Just stood there for twenty minutes.

Stache set the pages down. Let the ache settle.

Then he flipped to the sketch.

It was the house where they grew up. Back in western North Carolina. Gravel driveway. Broken mailbox. The tree was a maple he used to climb as a boy, long before he ever held a rifle.

The tree looked like it leaned a little.

Like it missed him.

The next morning, the squad assembled for a light run. Stache joined them. First time in weeks.

The air was thinner than usual. Or maybe it was just him.

Foster ran beside him, quiet.

"You always this fast, Sergeant?"

"Only when I've got ghosts chasing me."

Foster laughed softly. "Well, I guess I better keep up then."

They looped the perimeter once, then twice. On the third, Stache paused at the overlook.

The mountains stared back.

He remembered sitting in that same spot ten years earlier—except then it wasn't Afghanistan. It was Appalachian backcountry. ROTC field exercise. That's when he first knew he was meant to lead. Not because he wanted to. But because others would follow him even when the map didn't make sense.

Now he had a different map. A different kind of compass. One built on grief, trust, scripture, and fire.

The ghosts chased him more often these days. Faces he didn't save. Voices from convoys that never made it back. A friend who cracked a joke a minute before his truck exploded. A corporal who said, "I'll be right back," and never was.

Sometimes, they were louder than the firefights.

Back at the tent, Stache found Perez scribbling something into a spiral notebook.

"What's that?" he asked.

Perez shrugged. "Trying to write something my kid might read one day. Just in case."

Stache nodded. He understood.

He returned to his cot, reached for the envelope from last night, and placed it carefully into his Bible—tucked just behind Psalm 121.

The Lord will keep you from all harm—he will watch over your life.

No missions today. No gunfire.

Just a squad, a sky full of weight, and a little peace for once.

Stache lay back.

Outside, the wind passed over the valley like a prayer too soft to hear.

Chapter 8: Route Vulture

They called it Route Vulture. Narrow, winding, and flanked by cliffs on one side and sharp drops on the other. A logistical nightmare and an ambusher's dream. Which meant it was just another Tuesday.

Staff Sergeant Michael "Stache" Anderson stood beside the lead Humvee, the smell of fuel and metal heavy in the air. His breath fogged as he briefed the squad in the predawn dark.

"Today's route takes us through Vulture Pass to FOB Razor. One drop. High value—satcom gear, encrypted drives, and medical pallets. Rat truck takes the point. Gun trucks front and rear. Three cargo vehicles. No reroute options past klick twenty-five."

He flipped his clipboard.

"Resources: No EOD. MEDEVAC is limited— only one bird on standby for the entire region. QRF is delayed with another mission. If we get hit, we handle it. Aide and litter team is Jimmy and Foster. Ry, you're driving truck two. Perez stays on comms."

He let it settle in.

"Remember—only one way in. No way out but through."

The convoy rolled out with dust and diesel trailing behind. Route Vulture lived up to its name. Every bend felt like a blind leap. Rocks fell intermittently from the heights above, and the wind funneled through the pass with a banshee howl.

Stache kept his eyes moving. He'd been on edge since they left the gate. Something about today felt wrong.

Johnny's voice came through the radio. "Saw something glint on the ridge. Might be glass, might be optics."

"Copy. Gun trucks hold ready. Keep eyes high."

They made it fifteen klicks before the first sign of trouble. A herd of goats—untended, standing in the middle of the pass.

That was never good.

"Rat truck halt," Stache ordered. "Everyone else hold position. Alpha 3-4, dismount and scan."

The infantry team moved out with practiced caution.

Minutes passed.

Then chaos.

A deafening boom ripped the morning apart. The ground beneath truck three convulsed violently, like the earth had hiccupped in fury. The blast lifted the vehicle nearly five feet off the ground before slamming it back onto its side with a sickening crunch of metal and screaming rubber.

Flames burst from the undercarriage. Debris rained down—mud, twisted steel, fragments of armor plating. The concussive wave punched through the air, rattling every windshield in the convoy.

"TRUCK THREE DOWN! We've been hit!"

Inside truck three, the world went red and black. Windows spiderwebbed. A plume of black smoke rose like a signal flare, thick and fast.

"GUN TRUCKS—suppress left ridge!" Stache barked.

Small arms fire erupted from the rocks. AKs and something heavier—maybe a PKM. The pass became a kill zone. Rounds pinged against armor. Shards of rock exploded around the cargo trucks.

"Perez! Get me medevac on station! Jimmy, Foster—go!"

Smoke grenades burst orange and green as the litter team moved under fire.

The two infantrymen from Alpha 3-4 were already engaging, pushing fire toward the ridge to keep heads down.

Stache grabbed the mic.

"Red Two, initiating 9-line medevac:

Line 1: Grid 3150 3955

Line 2: Red Two, freq 36.95

Line 3: Three urgent

Line 4: None

Line 5: Litter—three

...Pause...

Line 6: Blast injuries, one with suspected spinal trauma

Line 7: None

Line 8: U.S. Military

Line 9: Orange smoke on mark."

"Copy Red Two. Dustoff en route. ETA six minutes."

Perez stayed low, feeding updates to command. Jimmy dragged the first casualty—unconscious, bleeding heavily from the head—clear of the wreckage. Foster worked a tourniquet into place on the second, whose leg was nearly mangled beyond recognition.

The third soldier, a gunner, was pinned inside. The turret ring had collapsed around his lower body. Stache was there in seconds, prying at the twisted hatch with bare hands.

"We can't cut him out here," Foster said, eyes wide.

"We don't," Stache growled. "We lift."

Together, three men heaved the frame just enough. The gunner screamed as they pulled him free, but he was alive.

The bird arrived low and hot, blades tearing the air. Dust and smoke whipped through the valley like a storm. Medevac medics sprinted from the ramp.

All three casualties were lifted under fire.

The bird lifted off hard and fast, banking wide.

Then it was gone.

That night, back at the FOB, the squad was quiet.

The three wounded had survived. One would be flown to Germany. The others would stay.

Stache stood over the wreckage of truck three, now hauled back to the yard. The frame was mangled. Inside, a single photo was still taped to the dash—Jimmy had placed it there months ago. A Polaroid of the whole squad, arms over shoulders, tired smiles, dust on every face.

Stache peeled it off, cleaned the soot away, and slipped it into his chest pocket.

Later, in the chapel, he sat alone again.

But this time, he prayed out loud.

Not for victory.

Not for vengeance.

Just for mercy.

And maybe—just maybe—for rest.

Chapter 9: False Calm

The mission was simple on paper—recovery and resupply. Nothing flashy. No major drops, no sensitive cargo. Just fuel, ammo crates, and cold-chain meds for a remote aid station tucked near the edge of the Pakistani border. But Stache had learned to fear the simple ones the most.

Convoys didn't die in the complex—they bled out in routine.

By 0500, trucks were staged and grumbling under their own weight. The mountain air smelled like frost and cordite. Stache stood next to his vehicle, thumbing through the updated manifest, mentally checking off every pallet, can, and ration.

"Today's route is Falcon Spur. No confirmed enemy presence, but recent drone footage picked up thermal signatures near grid 3246. Could be goat herders. Could be more. Assume they're watching," he said.

He flipped to the resource section.

"No EOD again. QRF is thirty mikes out minimum. MEDEVAC on standby with one bird—Stingray 4-2. Aide and litter is Perez and Foster today. Johnny's back on point. Gun trucks are staggered—two front, one rear."

He looked up.

"Don't let the word 'resupply' dull your edge. This road's tighter than a wrench on a cold bolt. You lose focus, you'll roll us into a ravine or worse."

They rolled out just after sunrise. The road wound along a narrow ridgeline, barely wide enough for a Humvee in some stretches. Each tire crunch seemed to echo off the rock face.

The convoy snaked down into the lower valley, dust hanging in the air like mist. Frost still clung to the shaded side of the road. The terrain here was dry but deceptive—thin crusts over soft patches that could suck a wheel like quicksand.

Truck two hit a dip hard enough to rattle everyone's teeth.

"Suspension's whining," Ry called over the radio. "Feels like the front driver's side is dragging."

Stache keyed up. "Copy. Keep eyes on it. If you lose power steering, call it early."

Then a crack—not gunfire. Mechanical.

Truck two jolted, veered hard left, and stopped dead. The convoy halted behind it.

"Red Two, front axle's fractured. We're stuck."

Stache jumped down and jogged up the line. The tire had caved under the frame—metal twisted like ribbon.

He muttered under his breath, "Too clean. That wasn't wear and tear."

Perez crouched down, brushing away the roadside debris. His hand stopped.

"Sir... there's scoring in the asphalt. Metal-on-metal."

Stache's gut tightened. He knelt and ran a gloved finger over it. Not natural. Something had scraped, maybe even cut. Premature sabotage?

He looked up. "Johnny. Get overwatch high and rear. Jimmy, reposition your gun truck and rotate 180. Lock down this road."

"Perez," he added, "call in a SITREP. Keep it vague—possible mechanical compromise."

The hours ticked by slower than usual.

A recovery team rolled out from the main FOB, dragging an armored tow rig behind a dusty 5-ton. While they waited, the squad fanned out in overwatch positions, scanning the ridgelines.

Stache walked the full 300 meters of the surrounding terrain himself. Climb. Scan. Breathe. Repeat.

He found two spent cigarette butts near a low ledge—Afghan brand. Still warm.

Whoever was up here, they'd been close. Watching. Maybe waiting. Maybe deciding whether today was worth it.

The truck was hauled out by 1430. No contact. No casualties.

But it felt worse than a firefight. It was the kind of silence that hid knives.

Back at base, Stache typed his log.

Mission: RESUPPLY/RECOVERY

Convoy: 6 vehicles

Route: Falcon Spur

Outcome: Partial mechanical failure (truck two)

Anomalies: Potential road sabotage — under review

He stared at the last line for a while.

Eventually, he added:

Recommend increased UAV sweep prior to future runs. Suggest engineering recon to inspect surface stability.

He leaned back, eyes bloodshot, throat dry.

Another simple run that wasn't.

And the ghosts weren't always loud.

Sometimes, they were quiet.

Sometimes, they were patient.

But they never stopped watching.

Chapter 10: The Long Haul

They'd been rolling for almost 36 hours.

Convoy 17 had stretched across two full days, two FOBs, and more miles of busted Afghan road than anyone wanted to count. The trucks were groaning, the men worse. Even the gunner in truck five—usually singing or talking trash—had gone quiet hours ago.

It was day two of a multi-FOB supply chain, and morale was starting to wear thin.

Staff Sergeant Michael "Stache" Anderson stood with a steaming mug of instant coffee at a small temporary TOC pitched against the wind-blown side of a mud wall compound. They had stopped for a planned refit and rest at a mid-route logistics point, a checkpoint called Camp Viper—barely more than a radio antenna, a fuel bladder, and a tent.

Morning briefing began before light broke.

"Last run through Falcon Spur revealed scoring on the asphalt. Could've been sabotage. If it wasn't, the wear patterns suggest active observation along the pass," Stache said, pointing to a map stretched over a folding table.

"Thermal drones last night picked up heat signatures in the rocks above checkpoint 6. We believe enemy observers may be leapfrogging us along ridgelines."

He paused.

"New intel says potential VBIED movements near grid 3392, intersecting our final stretch to FOB Castor. If we encounter a blockade, we do not approach. Jimmy, you're designated to punch through if needed—ram first, questions later."

The squad absorbed the information with tired eyes but steady resolve.

By 0630, the convoy rolled again. The air was colder, sharper. Engine growls and gravel spits the only rhythm left.

They climbed a steep ascent that had no guardrails, just a thousand-foot drop into God's memory. Every driver's knuckles were white on the wheel.

Around 0900, truck four reported engine temp spikes.

Stache answered over comms, "Back it down to half throttle. Bleed the heat slow. If we lose you, we're stuck until dark."

"Roger that. Truck four rolling limp."

An hour later, the sky turned brown.

Dust storm.

Visibility dropped to thirty feet. Headlights glowed like ghost eyes in the dirt haze. The column tightened formation, but risked spacing violations if ambushed.

Stache's voice cut through the net.

"No one brakes unless ordered. Rat truck keeps pushing. We'll ride the wall if we have to."

Inside the cabs, soldiers coughed through shemaghs and dry-throated curses. The smell of oil and sweat thickened.

Foster shifted in his seat. "This feels like a setup."

Stache didn't disagree. He just didn't say it out loud.

At 1132, the silence broke.

"Visual on vehicle ahead. Static. No movement." Johnny's voice was taut. "Mid-road, no heat coming off it."

"Could be a VBIED."

Stache didn't hesitate. "Jimmy, drive through. Everyone else, brace."

Truck three surged forward. Jimmy rammed the nose of their cargo rig into the side of the disabled vehicle, spinning it toward the slope. It toppled slowly, scraping against rocks, and tumbled out of sight.

No explosion.

But it had been real.

Pressure plate—underneath.

Johnny called it out. "Saw it last second—metal glint under the front axle."

No time for second guesses.

"Push through," Stache said. "Five klicks to FOB Castor."

They arrived caked in dust and silence. No one said much. Not about the fake car. Not about how close it had been.

In the motor pool, they parked in line. Exhaust hissed. Engines ticked.

Stache made the rounds.

"You good?" he asked Perez.

"Yeah," Perez nodded. "But that dust storm—felt like the desert was watching."

Stache patted his shoulder and moved on.

Inside the TOC, he scribbled into the logbook.

Mission: MULTI-DAY SUPPLY

Route: Falcon Spur > Castor Line

Incidents: Suspected VBIED decoy + pressure plate confirmed

He stared at the page.

Outcome: All personnel accounted for. Supplies delivered.

Condition: Fatigued, but operational.

Outside, the sun finally broke through the dust.

It didn't feel warm.

Chapter 11: Weight and Water

The trucks sat idle for once.

No mission. No movement. Just maintenance, inventory, and a full twelve hours of mandated rest at FOB Castor. For most soldiers, it was a luxury. For Staff Sergeant Michael "Stache" Anderson, it was a liability.

Still, even machines needed downtime. His squad definitely did.

It was late morning and already hot. The kind of heat that didn't just burn—it pressed. The sun blazed down like punishment from above. The gravel shimmered. Sweat soaked through uniforms even while standing still.

Inside the shade of a maintenance tent, Jimmy, Ry, and Foster were stripping down truck four's rear panel for an inspection. One of the bolts had sheared off after the last climb. Johnny was perched in the turret of the rat truck, watching the ridgeline even though no one had ordered him to.

Stache watched from the shadows.

He carried a canteen in one hand, a small notebook in the other. Inside were notes from every mission: time stamps, route anomalies, medevac logs, even dumb things like how often truck three needed coolant. It wasn't required. No one had asked for it. But it was his ritual—his way of remembering the details others overlooked.

Perez approached, wiping his face with a rag. "You see Foster this morning?"

"He was on the fuel run with supply."

Perez nodded. "Didn't say much. Took his rifle with him."

Stache frowned.

He found Foster sitting near the wire, not far from the east-facing guard tower. Helmet off, rifle across his lap, eyes on the hills.

"You're not on shift," Stache said as he approached.

Foster didn't look back. "I know."

Stache crouched beside him. They sat in silence for a while, listening to the wind brush against the sandbags.

"You've been quiet since the last run."

"It was the kid," Foster said. "I saw him."

Stache said nothing.

"He ran out from behind the wrecked car just as Jimmy hit it. We didn't see him again. No body. No movement. But I saw his eyes, Sergeant. Just for a second."

Stache exhaled slowly.

"Sometimes they use kids," he said finally. "Sometimes they don't. And sometimes... we'll never know which it was."

Foster nodded.

"I just keep thinking—what if I had yelled? What if I had radioed sooner?"

"That's how the ghosts get in," Stache said. "They don't kick the door down. They whisper 'what if.'"

That afternoon, he gathered the squad near the trucks under a camo net for shade. Instead of a formal brief, he sat on a crate.

"We've got forty-eight hours before our next push," he said. "Use it. Sleep. Write. Call home. This war isn't going anywhere."

They nodded. Nobody said much.

Then Ry opened a box.

"Got a care package from my sister. Homemade jerky and some nasty powdered Gatorade. Enough for everyone."

The mood lifted. Laughter returned. The kind that only comes in moments between chaos.

Later that evening, Stache stood outside his tent with a cup of warm bottled water. He looked out at the hills; the same ones Foster had been watching.

The desert was still.

For now.

He sipped the water slowly.

And whispered a verse he hadn't thought of in years:

"Whoever drinks of the water that I will give him will never be thirsty again..."

The heat didn't ease. The ghosts didn't leave.

But for a little while, the weight felt lighter.

Chapter 12: Thunder Without Warning

The silence didn't last.

Twelve hours into their mandated downtime, with the sun dipping behind the ridgelines and shadows crawling across the compound walls, FOB Castor was hit.

It started with a hollow thump. Distant. Muted. Like someone dropping a barrel far away.

Then came the whistle.

Then came the first impact.

The mortar struck just outside the motor pool, sending a geyser of rock and dirt into the air. It ripped a chunk from the wall, knocking over the makeshift fuel bladder and coating the nearby trucks in a haze of dust and debris.

Stache had been writing in his notebook, boots up on a cooler, when the blast hit. The concussion lifted him off the seat and slammed him against the side of a water tank.

"INCOMING!" someone screamed.

The alarm klaxon blared late. Too late.

Another round hit fifty meters from the comms tent.

He scrambled to his feet, ears ringing, dust choking his vision. Soldiers ran for cover. Some dove into the reinforced bunkers. Others ducked behind HESCO barriers, boots skidding on gravel.

"MOVE! GET TO COVER!" Stache bellowed, grabbing Foster by the collar as the younger soldier froze mid-sprint.

They dove behind the nearest concrete barrier just as another round landed, closer this time. The shockwave rattled the bones.

"Sound off!" Stache yelled into the net.

"Jimmy—green!"

"Ry—green!"

"Perez, I'm good!"

"Johnny—got eyes on the ridge. Looks like two-man spotter team. East slope, just under the saddle."

"Foster—green," the voice finally came, shaky.

The fourth mortar came screaming in. It hit the far edge of the barracks. Flames burst from the impact site. Screams followed.

"MEDIC! WE NEED A MEDIC!"

Stache grabbed his radio. "This is Red Two! FOB Castor under indirect fire—grid 3188 4061. Four impacts confirmed. Barracks hit. We have wounded. Request QRF support and immediate counter-battery fire. Over."

"Copy, Red Two. Artillery fire mission en route. QRF scrambling from Razor. Hold defensive posture."

But "holding" under falling sky wasn't easy.

Minutes dragged. Then the base's own mortars fired back. The boom shook the sandbags under Stache's boots. The retaliation was fast and precise. Somewhere on that ridge, the enemy was scattering or burning.

Then silence again.

Not peace—just the space between storms.

Stache ran with Foster and Perez to the barracks. Smoke poured from the roof; the corner wall nearly gone. Inside, two soldiers lay on the floor— shrapnel wounds and burns. Doc Matthews, bandaged but back on light duty, was already applying pressure.

"Help me with this one!"

They worked fast. No room for hesitation.

Litter teams carried both out as the fire teams doused the flames.

Later, after the chaos settled and the wounded were stabilized, Stache stood beside the rubble with Johnny.

"They got close," Johnny said, eyes on the still-smoking crater.

"They'll try again," Stache replied.

Johnny nodded. "Yeah. But so will we."

That night, nobody slept.

The squad sat in the motor pool under a pale moon, eating cold MREs and sipping from dented canteens. No jokes this time. No music. Just heavy silence.

Foster held his helmet in his lap like it might float away.

"You think they were watching us all day?" he asked.

Stache didn't answer right away.

Then he said, "Always."

He looked out past the perimeter.

The hills were darker than usual.

And somewhere out there, someone was already loading the next mortar.

Chapter 13: Blood and Bearings

Dawn came late.

Not because of clouds, but because no one was watching for it.

The squad moved like ghosts through the early hours, eyes sunken, uniforms streaked with ash and sweat. The barracks still smoldered in places, the wall scorched and cracked. Engineers had cordoned off the crater, but it felt more like a wound than a crime scene.

Staff Sergeant Michael "Stache" Anderson sat alone in the makeshift chapel, fingers laced tight over his Bible, head bowed—not in prayer, but in stillness. He hadn't slept. None of them really had.

At 0630, Captain Laura Smith called a command brief. Stache met her in the command tent, standing before a folding table cluttered with satellite imagery, half-empty coffee mugs, and dirt-streaked maps.

"We're not waiting," she said. "We're sending a hard push northeast toward OP Calypso. QRF's already mobilizing. You're taking point with the resupply column. If they try again, we end it."

Stache nodded. "What's the cargo?"

"Ammo. Rations. And med supplies. Some of it's for us, some of it's for the ANA detachment holding Calypso. They're stretched thin."

"Intel on contact?"

Smith glanced at the printout. "Thermals picked up movement four clicks east of your route. Could be ghosts. Could be the same team that spotted for last night's strike."

Stache looked at the grid. It was close. Too close.

"I want the option to deviate if we spot signs of prep."

"Granted. But this can't fail."

"It won't."

The squad gathered behind the trucks. The mood was grim, stripped bare of banter. Dust and fatigue hung on everyone's shoulders like second gear.

Stache stood in front of them.

"Listen up," he said. "This isn't just another run. We're carrying lifelines and pushing toward where the fire came from. If they hit us, we hit back harder. If we lose a truck, you know the drill. Recover, extract, push through. No hesitation."

He looked at Foster, who met his gaze with something steadier than before.

"Today, we ride for the ones who couldn't get out of that barracks. We ride for each other."

Johnny grunted. Jimmy nodded. Even Ry, usually deadpan, tapped his fist against the armored door before climbing in.

They rolled out before sunrise.

The road north wasn't marked on most maps—just a scratch of gravel and dust between switchbacks and ghost towns. The Humvees rattled with every dip. The rat truck, now rearmed with fresh optics and a new radio relay, led the column like a bloodhound.

By 0740, they reached the halfway point. Stache called a halt.

The convoy paused near a natural choke—two cliff walls forming a narrow pass. The kind of place that made good men nervous.

Johnny's voice crackled through. "Got heat bloom on thermal. Top ridge, west side."

"Copy. Eyes on. Gun one rotate and scan."

Nothing moved. The ridgeline stayed still.

Then came the burst.

A single RPG screamed across the sky, slamming into the rear gun truck. The impact shredded the rear axle and flipped the turret sideways.

"AMBUSH! REAR CONTACT!"

Stache's instincts kicked in. "Gun trucks lay down fire! Forward units, push through! Get clear of the kill zone!"

Bullets raked the convoy from the high ground. Stache's Humvee rocked as rounds pinged off armor.

"Foster, Ry, get to the rear! Pull them out! Jimmy, you're on fire lane left. Johnny, find their flank!"

The valley lit up. Rifle fire snapped across the rocks. The squad moved like muscle memory—training overriding terror.

Foster reached the burning gun truck, coughing through the smoke, and dragged the wounded gunner out by the straps of his plate carrier. Ry covered him, rifle steady.

"Red Two, this is Gun Three—we're mobile. Casualty stable. Returning suppressive!"

Stache keyed his mic. "Good work. Hold your lane. Dustoff is on standby if needed. No one dies here today."

They fought for seven minutes. Long enough to feel like seventy.

Then it stopped.

Silence dropped like a hammer.

The ambushers had scattered. Smoke still rose from the shattered rock face.

The convoy re-formed. Bloodied, but unbroken.

They rolled into OP Calypso at 1032. Dust-covered. Hearts heavy. Eyes sharper than before.

Stache stepped down from the truck and looked out over the wire.

The hills no longer looked empty.

He knew better now.

And so did they.

Chapter 14: The Weight He Carries

Private First Class Foster had never met anyone like Staff Sergeant Anderson.

It wasn't just the beard, or the gravel-in-his-gut voice, or even the way he stood like he'd been carved out of steel. It was how he carried the silence. How he moved through chaos like it was a routine formation. How he knew exactly where every man should be, even when the world was on fire.

Foster sat on an ammo crate near the back of the motor pool, watching Stache from across the compound. The sergeant was walking the perimeter again, checking gaps in the HESCO, talking to the tower guards, inspecting the battered convoy trucks. No one had ordered him to. No clipboard in hand. Just instinct.

And weight.

They all felt it, sure. The mortar strike. The ambush. The blood on their gloves and the ringing that wouldn't leave their ears. But Stache carried something else. A kind of responsibility that ran deeper than rank.

He remembered the first day he met the man.

Back in the States—Fort Bliss, Texas. Foster had arrived fresh from AIT, boots still factory clean and rucksack packed tighter than his nerves. The company office had been a blur of voices, papers, and unfamiliar faces. But Stache had stood out instantly.

He hadn't barked orders or sized him up with a hard stare. Instead, he'd stepped forward, offered a firm handshake, and said, "Welcome to the real world, Private. You bring your integrity, and I'll teach you everything else."

Foster had nodded, stiff and awkward.

Then Stache had done something he'd never expected: he took Foster out to the motor pool. Just the two of them. No checklist. No shouting. Just walking the line of Humvees, explaining how each truck had a story, how each one was more than steel—it was responsibility. Lives were attached to those bolts and belts.

"I don't care how good you shoot, Private," Stache had said, resting a hand on the hood of a desert-faded M1151. "You want to lead someday? Learn how to show up when nobody's watching."

Foster hadn't understood the full meaning then.

But now—after the convoys, the gunfire, the moments when everything balanced on one decision—he did.

"Why do you look at him like that?" Perez asked, sitting down beside Foster and tossing him a bottle of warm water.

Foster shrugged. "Because he's the kind of man you follow, even if you're not sure you'll make it back."

Perez nodded. "Yeah. He's carried all of us, one way or another."

They sat in silence a while longer.

From the corner of his eye, Foster saw Stache walk toward the small chapel—the same one that had survived two direct hits. He paused at the door, looked up at the darkening sky, and stepped inside.

Later that evening, Stache returned to the squad. No speeches. No rally cries. He just sat down next to the fire barrel where they were warming MREs.

"Tomorrow we run another route," he said plainly. "New maps come in at 0500. Get what sleep you can."

And that was that.

But to Foster, those words meant everything. Because if Stache said they'd get through tomorrow, then they would.

Because Stache didn't deal in promises—only in presence.

And that presence was enough to keep them together.

Even when the valley tried to tear them apart.

That night, long after most of the squad had turned in, Stache moved from bunk to bunk, cot to cot, checking in with each man quietly.

He paused at Ry's tent flap. "How's the shoulder?"

"Still sore," Ry muttered. "But I'll be fine by morning."

"Make sure of it. I'll have Perez ride in the second truck just in case."

At Jimmy's cot, Stache dropped an extra pair of earplugs and didn't say a word. Jimmy nodded, already half asleep but aware.

He stopped beside Foster last. The young private sat writing in his notebook, the firelight catching the edge of his pen.

"You ready?" Stache asked.

Foster looked up and didn't hesitate. "Yes, Sergeant."

Stache gave a small nod, one that carried more weight than any salute.

Then he turned back toward the shadows, boots crunching gravel with purpose, knowing tomorrow wasn't promised—but ready all the same.

Chapter 15: Dust in the Gears

The wind kicked up early.

By 0430, the dirt lot outside the FOB was already swirling with sand and static, ghosting through the beams of the Humvees' headlights. The morning was loud with the familiar clang of tailgates dropping, fuel pumps sputtering, and boots thudding against packed ground.

Stache stood near the lead vehicle, helmet under one arm, thermos in the other. His eyes scanned the convoy manifest as Perez ran final radio checks. Nothing had kicked off yet—but the tension in the air was as clear as the grit in their teeth.

The route ahead was called Route Saber—a jagged back trail not often used. Command had rerouted them last-minute to avoid suspected Taliban checkpoints to the south. That meant less intel, tighter choke points, and more places for something to go wrong.

"Today's run takes us west to FOB Ironhook," Stache said, briefing the squad. "New drop. Five trucks, two-gun mounts, Johnny leads in the rat. Foster and Jimmy in three. I'll be in two with Ry. We've got med crates, generators, and a sensitive electronics container for SATCOM—they want it intact."

He let the words settle before adding, "No confirmed threats, but Castor's last recon drone picked up a dug-in position two klicks off Saber. Could just be shepherds. Or a staging site."

They knew better than to assume the best.

The convoy pulled out at 0510.

The sun was just brushing the horizon when the first hour passed in relative quiet. Foster rode shotgun in truck three, chewing the inside of his cheek. He couldn't shake the feeling from the night before—Stache moving from bunk to bunk, checking on them, never saying much. Just being there.

That image grounded him more than the armor plating around the cab.

The road turned rocky fast. Saber didn't wind—it bucked. Potholes and washouts beat the suspension like a drumline.

At the two-hour mark, Johnny's voice cracked in over the net.

"Possible obstruction ahead. Metal, partially buried—looks fresh. Could be trash. Could be a decoy."

Stache responded instantly. "Copy. Halt movement. Gun one, cover left. Rat truck dismount. Get eyes on."

Foster watched in the side mirror as Johnny and his gunner approached the object—two meters long, rusted, jagged ends. They moved slow, methodical.

Then came the click.

A small one. Just enough.

Then the blast.

The explosion wasn't massive, but it didn't have to be. It lifted the front end of the rat truck and sheared the axle. The concussion cracked the air like thunder. Dirt rained like hail.

"AMBUSH IN PROGRESS!" Jimmy yelled. "Right ridge—six o'clock!"

Gunfire burst from the rocky hillside. AKs and a lone RPG screamed down.

"GUN TRUCKS—engage! Push suppressive on right ridge!" Stache's voice was ice and steel.

Inside truck three, Foster fumbled for his rifle.

"You good?" Jimmy shouted.

"Yeah," Foster said, pulling himself together. "Let's cover the rat."

They dismounted fast, crawling low. Stache was already out of truck two, directing the fire pattern, steady and brutal.

Rocks chipped. Dirt flew. Then, slowly, the fire began to falter.

Johnny's voice, hoarse but alive, came through. "Truck's out, but we're okay. Two wounded— minor."

"Foster, Ry—extract their crew. We're gonna tow the frame out. If it rolls, it rides. If not, we leave it."

Ten minutes of noise. Then stillness.

They reached Ironhook at 1043.

Four trucks whole. One limping. Squad intact.

Foster stood beside the towed rat truck, hands black with grease and soot. Stache approached, looked at the damage, then looked at him.

"You did good today."

Foster straightened. "We followed your lead."

Stache nodded once, then moved off toward the TOC without another word.

That was the thing about Stache. You never saw him trying to be in charge.

He just was.

And when the gears of war ground loudest, he was the only one who never buckled.

Chapter 16: Chain of Command

First Sergeant Carlton Briggs didn't knock. He kicked the TOC door open with his boot, dropped a folded map onto the steel table, and stared at the captain like he was deciding whether to argue or obey.

Captain Laura Smith didn't flinch. She looked up from her satellite overlays and met his stare.

"We're stretched thin. Again," Briggs said. "Ironhook's running short on batteries, water resupply is delayed two days, and I've got three-gun trucks down for axle repairs. And you want another patrol pushing east?"

Smith stood, straightening her blouse. "Not a patrol. A recon escort. Two ANA officers are coming down from Kunar to evaluate logistics corridors. They need American muscle to make it believable."

Briggs scoffed. "And who are you sending to play 'bodyguard with benefits'?"

Smith tapped the folder at the edge of the desk. "Second Platoon. Stache's team. They're already on location. Ironhook reported clean delivery, high morale, no casualties."

"Of course they are," Briggs muttered. "Because Anderson's not a soldier—he's a damn machine."

Lieutenant Daniel Price stepped through the doorway just as Briggs finished his sentence. Barely twenty-six, newly pinned, and still polishing off the stiffness of ROTC.

"You talking about Stache again?" he asked.

Briggs turned, grunted. "Your squad leader's too good. Makes the rest of us look like idiots."

Price chuckled awkwardly. "He's not hard to follow. Just hard to understand. Doesn't talk much."

Smith cut in. "But he moves the needle. He gets results. We've got dozens of leaders who yell orders. I'll take the one who doesn't have to."

Briggs nodded reluctantly. "He still calls in every kill zone like it's a damn checklist. No fluff. No drama. Just: 'truck hit,' 'crew recovered,' 'reform on grid 3180.' Like clockwork."

"That's what makes him lethal," Smith said. "He fights with his mind first. Then with fire."

Price looked uneasy. "You really think this next run's clean?"

Briggs turned toward him, dead serious. "Nothing's ever clean. Especially not in Sector Echo."

Later that afternoon, the leadership circle gathered in the officer's briefing tent for the mid-deployment sync—marking the halfway point of their rotation.

Captain Smith, Briggs, Lt. Price, and Stache all sat around the center table. Unlike normal briefs, this one was looser in tone—fewer maps, more reflection.

Smith started. "We're at ninety days. We've lost two trucks. No KIA. Twelve wounded. We've completed every scheduled convoy, hit every checkpoint. That's not luck. That's leadership."

She turned to Stache.

"Talk to me. How's your platoon holding?"

Stache leaned forward. "They're tired, ma'am. Running lean. But they're bonded. Stronger than day one. Foster's grown fast. Jimmy's leading on the fly. Johnny doesn't say much, but he sees everything."

Briggs added, "I've seen 'em come back after firefights like it was a drill. No panic. Just process."

Price asked, "What about morale? They showing signs of fatigue?"

Stache nodded. "Some. Nightmares. Restless sleep. But they take care of each other. We've built rhythm. Mail helps. So do care packages. We had a scare after the mortar attack, but Foster's been checking in on the new guys. It matters."

Smith looked around the table. "We're halfway there. We hold this tempo, we come out sharper

86

than we went in. But no one gets complacent. You feel something slipping, say it early."

Stache spoke again. "I'll keep them tight. But I'll need support for truck three's engine and I want a fresh comms repeater. Signal's fading in the hills."

Briggs scribbled it down. "You'll have it by Friday."

Smith stood. "Alright. Next convoy steps at 0600. Escort, light armor, ANA delegation. We'll go over route Saber again in the morning."

As the group stood to leave, Smith pulled Stache aside.

"I read every one of your reports," she said. "You don't waste words. That's how I know you mean every one you use."

Stache gave a small nod. "They follow because they know I won't feed them false hope. Just the truth."

"That's leadership," Smith said. "Keep at it, Sergeant."

Back at FOB Ironhook, Stache stood over a table in the maintenance bay, sleeves rolled, grease smudged down both forearms.

He wasn't resting. He was checking wiring on the truck's radio relay, trying to figure out why their signal kept fading at ridge points. Johnny hovered nearby, watching, but not speaking.

A young staff specialist walked in, carrying a sealed envelope.

"Sir—message from Battalion. Tasking order. Says it's priority."

Stache took the envelope, opened it with his knife, and scanned the contents. His jaw tightened just slightly.

Foster walked in behind him, catching the tail end of the moment.

"Everything good?" he asked.

Stache folded the paper neatly, slid it into his cargo pocket.

"We've got a new assignment. Escort mission. VIPs. Light element. We step at 0600."

Foster blinked. "Another one?"

Stache didn't answer the question. Just picked up the radio wiring and went back to work.

Because leadership didn't come with explanations.

It came with example.

And the mission never stopped.

Chapter 17: Smoke and Smiles

0430 came with cold air and tired bones.

The squad moved in practiced silence; their movements efficient but heavy. MRE wrappers crinkled, boots laced tight, hands checking bolts and radios. The night hadn't offered much sleep— not with the new tasking looming and the weight of command tightening like a strap on Stache's chest.

The ANA officers were due to arrive by 0500. The escort route stretched deep into the Echo corridor, a region known for ambushes, washed-out trails, and comms dead zones. Stache didn't like the assignment. But he didn't say that out loud. He never did.

Perez jogged up, helmet under one arm.

"Gun trucks fueled and synced. Johnny's already running optics checks on the rat. We've got good spacing."

Stache nodded. "Load the medical container last. If we need to drop weight, we lose the crates—not the people."

By 0515, the ANA liaisons arrived. Two officers, a translator, and four infantrymen. Nervous smiles. Dusty uniforms. They were polite but clearly uneasy—especially after seeing how hard-edged and quiet Stache's team was.

One of the officers, Captain Hamid, stepped forward with a hand extended. "Staff Sergeant Anderson, yes?"

Stache shook his hand firmly. "That's right. You'll be in vehicle two, right behind the rat truck."

Hamid nodded. "We've heard about your team. Your soldiers—they stand fast."

"We move together," Stache replied. "No one gets left behind. That includes you."

The translator relayed it to the rest of the ANA detail, and a few nodded quietly, visibly reassured.

Lieutenant Price approached, clipboard in hand. "You've got overwatch and primary logistics security. They ride in the second truck. Gun one and rat lead out."

Stache nodded.

Before mounting up, he pulled the squad into a tight circle.

"No assumptions," he said, voice calm but firm. "We've had clean runs turn dirty, and bad ones go quiet. Keep spacing, stay alert. If we lose comms, fall back to grid check three and hold. If we get split—follow the last standing truck."

Eyes met his. They didn't need motivation.

They just needed direction.

The convoy rolled out under a rising sun.

The landscape stretched dry and cracked, ridgelines looming like teeth. Thirty minutes in, they reached a shallow basin where roads forked—one toward the known pass, the other toward Echo Ridge.

Stache keyed up. "Johnny, confirm thermal read."

"Nothing major. Just some heat on the ridge—small campfire. Might be civilian."

"Might not," Stache said. "Maintain course. No deviation unless fired upon."

As they crested the next hill, a sharp pop echoed.

Then another.

Not an IED.

Gunfire.

"Rear contact! Small arms! Approx. five shooters—elevated!" Perez's voice was sharp.

"Push forward!" Stache ordered. "Gun one, return fire and stagger right. Protect the ANA vehicle!"

Bullets peppered the left side of the convoy. One round cracked the window beside Foster's head.

The ANA troops dismounted without orders, returning fire from shallow cover. One took a round to the thigh and collapsed.

"Johnny, suppress ridge! Foster, get that man behind the engine block—go!"

Foster didn't hesitate.

He dragged the wounded ANA officer by the webbing, ducking rounds, heart thundering in his chest. Jimmy laid down cover fire as the gun trucks lit up the ridge.

Then—silence.

No retreat. Just absence.

The enemy had vanished back into the hills.

They reached the rally point an hour later.

The ANA officer was stable. The rest of the squad was intact.

After offloading the delegation, Stache took a few moments to debrief with Captain Hamid. They stood in the shade of the rat truck, drinking warm water and wiping dust from their faces.

"You stayed with us," Hamid said. "When the firing began... some Americans pull away. You stayed."

"We fight as one," Stache said.

Hamid nodded. "That means more to my men than you know. Thank you, Sergeant."

Later that afternoon, the squad was granted downtime before regrouping at FOB Ironhook.

They spread out across the gravel clearing beneath a ragged awning. No one spoke for a while. The quiet wasn't uncomfortable—it was earned.

Ry cleaned his rifle in silence. Perez wrote in a small green notebook. Jimmy and Foster sat cross-legged, trading war stories with one of the ANA infantrymen using broken English and animated hand gestures.

Johnny leaned against the wheel well, eyes half-shut but alert.

Stache stood off to the side, sipping a half-warm pouch of coffee, listening without intruding. Seeing his team not just surviving—but bonding, recovering, breathing—that was his reward.

Foster walked over with a grin. "They were showing us pictures of their families. One of the ANA guys has twin boys. Said he prays for them before every mission."

Stache nodded. "We all do. Whether we say it out loud or not."

The wind kicked up just then, tugging at the corners of the awning. A few laughed and swatted dust away.

In that moment, they weren't just a squad.

They were brothers.

And for the first time in days, the valley seemed quiet enough to let them feel it.

Chapter 18: Shadows Move Quietly

The wind had shifted by midnight.

It rolled in low and steady across the perimeter of FOB Ironhook, dry and dust-laden, carrying with it a smell that never quite settled—part earth, part engine oil, part something else. The kind of smell you remembered even after the tour was over.

Staff Sergeant Anderson couldn't sleep. He sat alone on the sandbags near the southern watchtower, rifle across his lap, helmet beside him, eyes on the horizon. The rest of the squad was out cold, their gear resting beside them in tight piles. Foster was curled up near the fire barrel, one boot still on. Jimmy had nodded off mid-sentence. Perez snored like a generator.

But something wasn't right.

Stache didn't know what it was yet, but he'd learned to trust the silence that followed good days. The kind that settled too easily.

Inside the TOC, Lt. Price tapped through sat feed updates while First Sergeant Briggs sipped from a dented canteen. Captain Smith leaned over the ops board, frowning.

"We've had too many soft days in Echo. I don't trust it," she muttered.

Briggs grunted. "The hills are breathing. You can feel it."

Price looked up. "Stache submitted a patrol overlay for the eastern route. Wants extra eyes around the ridgelines—he's requesting night drone support and a fire watch rotation."

Smith didn't hesitate. "Approved. Put eyes on his line."

At 0307, the first sensor tripped.

Perimeter wire, southeast corner. A low chime buzzed in the TOC. Then two more.

Motion.

Outside, the watchtower lights blinked on. Gun crews rustled to life.

Stache was already moving. Rifle in hand, vest half-buckled, boots pounding gravel.

"Perez, wake the squad!" he snapped. "Johnny, man the 240. Get elevation. Foster—eyes on the breach."

Foster shook off sleep like a weight, scrambled to the barrier line with his NVGs.

Through the green-tinted lens, he spotted movement.

Figures. Three, maybe four. Low, fast, shadowed. Not animals.

"Contact. Grid southeast 3-1-2. They're crawling. Maybe probing."

"Hold fire," Stache said. "They haven't committed."

He raised his radio. "Red Two to TOC. Possible recon team at wire. No shots fired. Watching for confirmation."

Smith's voice came back sharp. "Copy. QRF on standby. Drone en route."

The squad crouched low behind the barriers. Adrenaline filled the space where sleep had lived. Time stretched.

Then a shout.

One of the figures had risen too fast. Tripped wire. Flare.

Light bloomed over the valley.

Stache didn't hesitate. "Suppressive fire! Watch the flanks!"

The gun trucks came alive, barrels flashing. The hills lit up like fireflies.

The figures scattered. Return fire cracked from the ridge.

"Johnny, shift left! Ry—watch your lane!"

Perez tossed a smoke canister over the wire, clouding the path.

After five minutes, it was over.

Sunrise came late that morning.

The squad sat in silence, exhausted but wired. No casualties. Just close calls and frayed nerves.

Stache stood near the wire with Captain Smith.

"They were just testing us," she said.

"For now," he replied. "Next time they'll bring more."

She looked at him. "You holding up?"

Stache didn't answer. He didn't need to.

He was already looking out past the wire again.

The valley didn't rest.

So neither would he.

Because Stache knew the silence wasn't peace—it was the pause before the next trial. And in those moments, when the adrenaline wore off and the squad returned to their cots, he stayed up longer. Not because of fear. But because of faith.

He reached into his chest pocket and pulled out the small Bible he'd carried since basic. The cover was torn, smudged with dirt and oil. He flipped to Psalm 91—his anchor.

*"He who dwells in the shelter of the Most High will abide in the shadow of the Almighty. I will say

97

to the Lord, 'My refuge and my fortress, my God, in whom I trust.'"

Stache didn't pretend to have all the answers. But he trusted the One who did. Every mission, every moment spent behind the wheel or under fire—he gave it back to God. Not as a transaction. But as a surrender.

He'd learned long ago that strength came not from the armor he wore but from the Spirit within him. And as the sun finally broke over the ridgeline, he whispered the prayer he always returned to:

"Use me, Lord. However You see fit. I'll stand in the gap."

Then he buckled his vest again.

The next battle would come.

And he would meet it—not alone, but guided.

Chapter 19: Burned Roads

The call came in at 0415.

A convoy from Alpha Company had been hit along Route Dagmar—three vehicles disabled, unknown number of wounded, with one vehicle unaccounted for. QRF was mounting out of Razor, but the nearest support was Stache's squad. They were closest.

By 0430, Stache was on his feet and waking the others with calm urgency.

"Up and moving. This one's real."

The squad didn't need extra words. The quiet way Stache moved said enough.

Within minutes, they had gear stowed, weapons checked, trucks spooling to life. The air was cooler than expected, almost metallic.

Perez handed Stache the updated coordinates. "They're still taking sporadic fire. No air until daylight. We'll have to fight them out."

Stache nodded. "Let's roll."

Route Dagmar wasn't friendly to begin with. Cracked pavement gave way to sunbaked dirt, littered with broken culverts and the occasional burned-out shell of a fuel truck long forgotten.

The rat truck took lead. Johnny scanned the ridgelines, hyperaware. Foster kept his eyes locked on the treeline, sweat already creeping into his gloves.

They found the wreckage just after 0500.

Smoke still curled from the lead vehicle—an MRAP torn open from beneath, likely a pressure plate rig. The second truck was in a ditch, riddled with bullet holes. The third was nowhere to be seen.

Stache dismounted, hand up.

"Fan out. Move slow. Look for boot drag, casing scatter. We find our people."

They found the survivors 300 meters off the road, hunkered down in a dry irrigation trench. Three soldiers, one barely conscious from blood loss. Another was trying to rig a field IV using a canteen tube and tape.

Perez radioed the TOC. "Found them. Three alive. One critical. No eyes on missing vehicle."

Then came the crack of a rifle.

"CONTACT—east ridge!"

Gunfire ripped across the trench as Stache tackled the injured man, dragging him behind a burned tire mound. Johnny returned fire immediately, the turret hammering down range.

"Jimmy, Foster—cover left! Ry, get a smoke out! Perez—prep the litter!"

The firefight lasted nine minutes. A full eternity in that stretch of hell.

By the time they pulled out, the sun had risen, golden and indifferent.

They left tire tracks in blood and soot.

Back at Ironhook, the wounded were stabilized. The trench crew would live. The third truck was found hours later—empty, stripped, torched.

But it wasn't the truck that haunted them.

It was what they didn't find.

No bodies. No gear. No footprints leading away. The cab had blood—smears along the interior panel, a streak on the doorframe—but no sign of where the crew had gone. Not a single spent casing around the truck. Not a call for help over the net.

Intel later confirmed a new enemy tactic—capture over kill. A tactic meant to rattle nerves, erode confidence.

Captain Smith called for immediate drone surveillance of the region. QRF sweep teams were pushed out the next morning, but it was as if the desert had swallowed them whole.

Foster stared at the empty shell of the truck while they waited for the drone feed. "They were here… and then they weren't."

Stache stood beside him, silent for a long moment.

"Write their names down," he finally said. "They're not gone. They're just not back yet."

He didn't say it out of false hope.

He said it like a promise.

That night, Stache sat on the edge of a cargo pallet, alone.

He didn't speak. Just flipped his Bible to Proverbs 24:10.

"If you faint in the day of adversity, your strength is small."

He read it once. Then again.

Then he closed the book and stared at the horizon, where the wind hadn't stopped.

They were still in it.

But they were still standing.

Chapter 20: Pastoral Interlude

The morning after Dagmar was quieter than expected. Not silent—never that—but quieter. A kind of stillness that didn't come from peace, but exhaustion.

The squad had cleaned their rifles, reset their kits, and gone through the motions of a typical reset day. But none of it felt typical. Not after seeing what they saw. Not after finding a truck with no crew. Not after writing down names without answers.

By noon, Captain Smith had assembled the leadership team in the TOC. Stache stood near the edge of the folding table, arms crossed, jaw set.

"We need to prep for the next cycle," Smith said. "But morale is dipping—hard. And not just your squad. The whole line's been rattled. They're starting to ask questions."

Briggs, hunched over the patrol log, grunted. "Can't blame 'em. We've never had a truck go ghost before."

Price glanced toward Stache. "They're looking to your team. They see calm. Stability. That counts."

Stache finally spoke. "They don't need me to have the answers. They need to see me not break."

Smith nodded. "Good. Because that's what we're asking you to keep doing. We'll rotate your squad to FOB Sentinel for 48. Time away from the Echo zone. Let them breathe."

Briggs raised a brow. "A break?"

"Not a reward. A recalibration," Smith said. "They've carried the weight long enough. Let them drop it. Just for a while."

FOB Sentinel sat along a flat basin, ringed by rusted fencing and wind-beaten flags. It wasn't fancy. But it was quiet. No mortars. No movement on the wire. Just dry sun and time.

The squad stepped off the trucks like they were stepping into a different deployment.

Within hours, Perez was playing cards with a new crew. Jimmy found a weight bench under a canopy and started deadlifting in silence. Johnny napped under the tailgate with his boonie pulled low.

Foster climbed a ladder to the roof of the barracks and just sat.

And Stache walked the perimeter alone, as he always did—until the chaplain found him.

"Sergeant Anderson," the chaplain said, pacing beside him. "I hear your name often. Soldiers talk."

Stache gave a half glance. "Good or bad?"

The chaplain smiled. "They say you're the anchor when the waves get violent. They follow your silence."

Stache kept walking. "That silence isn't always strength. Sometimes it's the only thing I've got left."

The chaplain nodded slowly. "I've read Psalm 46 a lot lately. 'Be still and know that I am God.' Stillness isn't weakness, Stache. It's surrender. It's space for Him to speak."

They stopped near the wire.

Stache looked out across the empty plain.

"I stay strong for them. But some nights, I don't feel anything. No fear, no peace. Just... space."

The chaplain reached into his coat and handed him a worn slip of paper. It was folded four times and soft around the edges.

"My father carried this in Vietnam," the chaplain said. "He told me: 'When you can't feel God, remember that He never stopped watching.'"

Stache unfolded the paper. It was Isaiah 41:10:

"Do not fear, for I am with you. Do not be dismayed, for I am your God. I will strengthen you and help you; I will uphold you with my righteous right hand."

"I don't have many words to give," the chaplain added. "But that verse's carried more men through the valley than sermons ever could."

Stache stood silent for a moment longer.

Then he folded the paper gently, slid it behind the flap of his armor plate, and said, "Thanks, Chaplain."

"Anytime," the chaplain said. "Just don't forget—you don't have to carry it all. Even He didn't ask you to."

That night, for the first time in weeks, the squad laughed around a burn barrel. Foster told a story from basic. Perez swore it wasn't true. Jimmy made a plate of beef stew from two MREs and called it "field gourmet." Even Johnny smiled.

And Stache sat with them.

No Bible. No rifle. Just presence.

The mission would come again soon.

But for now, the dust had settled.

And they breathed.

Chapter 21: Innocent Eyes

The break at FOB Sentinel ended with a single phrase over the net:

"Echo corridor, grid 3319, fire mission ongoing. Request route clearance and QRF escort—hostile contact confirmed."

The valley was calling again.

Within twenty minutes, Stache's squad was mounted up, checked in, and back on the move. The brief silence of Sentinel faded behind them like a mirage, replaced by the rattle of suspension over gravel and the high drone of vigilance settling back over the team.

No one complained. No one needed to.

They were ready.

Route Bravo Tango ran through a high cut of switchbacks and shale, pinched between twin ridgelines that overlooked a narrow dirt artery barely wide enough for two vehicles side by side. Known to be ambush country. Too much elevation. Too many shadows.

Perez reviewed the overlay on his tablet. "We've got a drone in the area, but coverage is thin. They want us to confirm the route's clear for a mechanized unit inbound from Razor."

Stache nodded. "We go in slow. Gun mounts up. Rat truck two hundred out front. Johnny takes ridge right with eyes high."

The squad knew the drill.

They were an hour in when the ambush triggered.

Not with a boom—but with the shriek of a dismounted RPG streaking from the ridge.

"INCOMING—RIGHT FLANK!" Johnny shouted.

The lead Humvee swerved hard, the blast missing by inches and rocking the whole trail.

"CONTACT! MULTIPLE SHOOTERS— RIDGE LINE AND TREE COVER!"

The air turned to chaos—gunfire hammering from above, the crack and hiss of rounds whipping low. Stache issued orders through the net like a conductor with steel nerves:

"Jimmy—return fire uphill, arc left! Foster—cover Johnny's flank, pin their cut-off! Ry—smoke high, obscure our rear!"

The squad moved with lethal rhythm.

Even as bullets slapped metal and sparks flew off hoods, they held their formation, rotated angles, and kept pressing forward.

Stache dismounted when the third volley came in, moving up a rocky incline to get line of sight. He spotted muzzle flashes between a row of broken shrubs.

Then he heard it—a voice calling out in Pashto. Urgent, desperate. Not a war cry. Not even a warning.

A plea.

Stache pivoted, raising a closed fist to halt the squad's advance. Through the shifting dust, he saw the shape of a boy—maybe fifteen or sixteen— barefoot, panting, one hand in the air and the other waving them back.

"Hold," Stache said into the radio. "Repeat—hold your fire. Civilian on ridge."

The boy stumbled toward them, wide-eyed and shaking. Sweat and dust streaked his face. He kept repeating the same Pashto phrase over and over. Stache lowered his rifle, hands out in a calming gesture.

Perez translated quickly. "He says—'Don't shoot. They made me show the path. I didn't know you were close.'"

Stache's eyes locked on the boy's. "Is anyone else with them?"

The boy nodded. "Yes. Two. They go into the dark. The cave."

Stache looked up the ridge, then back at the boy. "Did you help them plant charges?"

The boy shook his head rapidly. "No. Only show them where the pass turns."

Perez stepped forward. "He says they threatened his sister if he didn't help."

There was a pause.

Stache's jaw tightened. "Give him water. Let him sit in the shade. We're not his enemy."

The boy sank to the ground, more from fear than fatigue.

"Perez—mark that ridge line. We've got cave structures. Hostiles retreating. Civilian spotted. Repeat—do not engage unless fired upon."

Stache didn't fire.

"Perez—mark that ridge line. We've got cave structures. Hostiles retreating. Civilian spotted. Repeat—do not engage unless fired upon."

The squad held fire. The enemy vanished again.

They made the ridge by noon. Route cleared. Contact broken.

Stache stood at the edge of the overlook, watching dust settle on the road below.

Foster approached quietly. "That kid saved us time. Could've walked into an ambush with half the team in open ground."

Stache didn't look away. "He was scared. Didn't want to see blood."

"Think he knew we'd hold back?"

Stache finally turned. "I think he hoped someone would."

That night, back at Ironhook, Stache flipped open his Bible to Matthew 5:9.

"Blessed are the peacemakers, for they shall be called sons of God."

He underlined the verse.

Then whispered, more to himself than anyone:

"Even in a valley of fire... we were still called to be one."

Chapter 22: Redeeming the Silence

The caves haunted Stache.

Not the ones carved in stone—but the ones left in memory. He couldn't stop thinking about the boy. About the way his hands shook. About how he hadn't run. About the terror in his voice that had nothing to do with bullets.

Two days after the firefight, Stache stood with Captain Smith in the TOC. Overlays and drone captures flickered across the screen. The caves were confirmed—deep, interconnected. Insurgents were staging from there, using locals to move gear and mislead convoys.

"They're embedding fear," Smith said quietly. "Not just tactics. Psychological pressure. They want our people to second guess the civilians."

Stache folded his arms. "I won't."

Smith looked at him. "Good. Because it's working in other units. But not yours."

Later that night, under the hiss of low wind, Stache sat with Foster near the rear of the motor pool. No fire barrel. No noise. Just two folding chairs and the weight of shared silence.

"He was just a kid," Foster said finally. "Like me, back when I didn't know anything. Except he got handed a rifle and a threat instead of a rucksack."

Stache nodded. "The enemy thinks fear is faster than faith."

"You think that kid had faith?"

"I think he had hope," Stache replied. "And sometimes that's what faith looks like when you've got nothing left."

Foster leaned back, exhaled. "You ever lose faith?"

Stache was quiet for a while. Then he pulled the folded paper from behind his armor plate. Isaiah 41:10.

"Every time I feel empty, I read this. And I remember—I'm not alone. Neither are you."

He paused, then glanced over at Foster. "Can I ask you something?"

Foster nodded. "Course."

"Where's your faith at, Foster? Not religion. Not check-the-box answers. But do you know where you stand with God?"

Foster looked at the gravel. "I don't know. I mean... I try to be good. I believe in something, I guess. Just never really thought I'd need to make it official."

Stache leaned forward. "Let me walk you through something. Something simple, but real. It's called the Romans Road. It helped me understand when I needed direction."

Foster listened intently.

"Romans 3:23—'For all have sinned and fall short of the glory of God.' That's all of us, man. No one here's got clean hands.

Romans 6:23—'For the wages of sin is death, but the gift of God is eternal life in Christ Jesus our Lord.' We earn death for our sin. But He gives life.

Romans 5:8—'But God demonstrates His own love for us in this: While we were still sinners, Christ died for us.' He didn't wait for us to get right. He came into the fire for us.

And Romans 10:9—'If you confess with your mouth, "Jesus is Lord," and believe in your heart that God raised Him from the dead, you will be saved.' That's it. No politics. No rank. Just surrender."

Foster's eyes welled slightly. "You think… you think He'd actually forgive someone like me?"

"I don't think," Stache said softly. "I know."

There was a long pause.

"Would you… pray with me?"

Stache nodded. "Right here. Right now."

They bowed their heads beneath the stars, the night quiet except for the distant hum of a generator.

Foster whispered a prayer that changed everything.

By the next morning, the squad was prepping for another movement. Another drop. Another unknown.

Before they rolled out, Stache gathered them near the trucks.

"I know you're tired," he said. "I know it feels like the same road every time. But it's not. Every road is new to someone. Every mile we hold safe means someone else gets to come home. So we go again. Because we're not just defending lanes—we're proving we're different."

The team nodded, silent but steady.

As they mounted up, Foster whispered to Perez, "I think we'll be okay."

Perez looked over. "Why?"

Foster smiled. "Because Stache still believes. And now… I do too."

And in a place where dust never settled long, that belief was enough to keep them moving forward.

Chapter 23: Transformation

The morning air hit colder than usual, a biting edge that slipped through gloves and found skin. It was the kind of cold that reminded every soldier they were alive—and how close they'd come to not being.

The convoy today was smaller. Recon and humanitarian aid. Food, water filters, and a mobile med kit packed into the back of truck two. They were headed into a valley just past the Echo Ridge caves—a village too small to mark on most maps.

"Population maybe fifty," Perez read from the brief. "Goats, kids, elders. No known hostiles. But no guarantees."

Stache had heard that line before.

They rolled out with a different air this time. Not less serious—never that—but steadier. Foster rode with a calm that hadn't been there a week ago. Something in him had shifted—not just mentally, but deep down where fear used to sit.

The weight he'd carried, the unseen burden of guilt and uncertainty, felt lighter. Not gone—this was still war—but it was no longer crushing. For the first time since arriving in-country, he didn't feel like he had to earn his worth every day. He wasn't fighting to prove something. He was moving with purpose.

He read from his pocket Bible on the way out, lips moving silently over verses he'd underlined the night before. Romans. Psalms. Ephesians. Each one felt like fuel.

He helped double-check gear without being asked, not out of routine, but out of love—for the men beside him, for the mission, and for the God who had seen him even in the dark.

Stache watched him with a quiet pride. Not the kind you boast about—but the kind that anchors a man.

The valley opened in a soft curve, hemmed in by red clay cliffs and low, scrubby trees. As they pulled in, villagers appeared slowly—faces cautious, eyes sharp. Children held back behind older women. One man stood at the front, unarmed, arms crossed over a faded green robe.

Stache dismounted first, hands visible, posture relaxed but alert.

"We're here to help," he said. "No force. No demands."

The interpreter relayed the message. A few villagers stepped forward. Within minutes, the squad was unloading supplies, setting up the med kit, and distributing clean water packets. Jimmy checked a child's infected foot. Perez fixed a solar panel that had fallen from a roof.

Foster handed out food and bent low to tie a toddler's shoe.

One old man approached him, whispering in broken English. "You are soldiers... but different."

Foster smiled. "We follow a different kind of Commander."

Stache watched from the edge of the village. He still scanned the ridge every two minutes. Still checked spacing. But he let himself breathe a little deeper.

Captain Hamid arrived mid-afternoon with two ANA soldiers. They had coordinated support drop-offs further down the ridge. Hamid greeted Stache with a nod of respect.

"You returned," he said.

"Always," Stache replied.

Hamid pointed to the squad. "They act like shepherds, not warriors."

Stache smiled. "Sometimes we're called to be both."

Before leaving, the elder of the village offered a carved wooden plate to the squad. Stache declined the gift, but Foster stepped forward.

"We can't take gifts," he said. "But we'll remember you."

The elder nodded. "That is enough."

That night, back at Ironhook, Foster wrote in a small notebook—something he hadn't done since his first week in-country. Across the top of the page, he wrote:

"Sometimes the mission isn't a fight. Sometimes it's just being willing to show up."

He closed the notebook, tucked it into his vest, and looked up at the stars.

Stache was already walking the wire.

Some things never changed.

And some things changed everything.

Chapter 24: A New Creation

By the third week of October, the dust had changed.

It wasn't just heavier—it clung to everything. Boots, belts, skin. Even in the folds of letters from home, smuggled in between missions, it settled like a reminder that war was still watching.

Stache knelt in front of truck four, hands buried in the suspension housing, checking bolts and cabling that had rattled loose on the last run. The motor pool was loud with maintenance, but his mind was quieter than usual.

He wasn't thinking about fuel lines or comms static.

He was thinking about Foster.

The kid had found something real. And it showed.

Not just in how he read Scripture before rack time, or the way he stopped swearing under stress, but in how he walked. His eyes were clearer. His steps had rhythm. Even Perez had noticed.

"Your shadow got lighter," he joked one night. "Like you stopped dragging something no one else could see."

Foster had just smiled.

The next mission came with layers.

A two-day haul north through broken terrain with limited overwatch and a promise of resistance. Two convoys would link mid-route and deliver joint supplies to a forward med station running low on pain meds and plasma.

Jimmy took lead. Foster drove rear. Stache stayed center with Perez and a sat relay that blinked more red than green.

The route wound through bone-dry creek beds and collapsed culverts. Nothing moved—not even the wind.

Halfway through day one, a call came over the net.

"Civilian down. Roadside. Ten meters off trail. No movement."

Foster keyed in. "I see him. Looks older. No weapon. May be hurt."

"Hold position," Stache ordered. "Let me approach."

Stache moved slow, rifle low, eyes scanning the ridgeline above. The man on the ground was bleeding from the leg, clutching a worn satchel. He looked up with fear and pain, muttering in Pashto.

The interpreter behind Stache translated. "He says he was caught in a firefight. Not with us. Taliban patrol. He ran."

Stache offered water. "We'll get you to safety."

The man gripped his hand with surprising strength. "You are not like them."

That night, the squad set up perimeter around the man as medics from the second convoy arrived. Foster knelt beside him while Perez logged comms data.

Earlier, during the long push through the creek bed, Jimmy had glanced over at Foster between bumps and dust clouds.

"Yo," Jimmy said, squinting. "You different lately."

Foster blinked. "Different how?"

"You don't flinch at the dark spots. Don't curse when we get bad news. And you're the first one to check the water packs. That's new."

Foster grinned. "I guess I finally figured out who's actually driving this convoy."

Jimmy laughed once. "Well, if He's got the wheel, remind Him this suspension sucks."

"He asked if we were Christians," Foster said.

"What'd you say?" Stache asked.

"I said yes. Then I told him... we were taught to love before we were taught to fight."

Stache nodded.

"Good."

That evening, the squad shared packets of apple cinnamon MREs and a moment of rare laughter under the stars. It wasn't perfect. The mission wasn't over. But something sacred had stirred beneath the grit and weight.

As Foster stared into the dark beyond the camp's glow, he whispered a prayer without fear.

He wasn't walking alone anymore.

And the road beneath him—dusty, cracked, and dangerous—felt holy.

Chapter 25: The Final Firefight

The storm didn't start with thunder.

It began with silence—an unnatural stillness that blanketed the camp the next morning. The wind had stopped, the usual background chatter gone. Even the birds had disappeared. It was the kind of quiet that tightened stomachs and made veterans glance twice at their rifles.

Stache felt it before anyone said a word. He stood near the wire, eyes scanning the ridgeline.

Perez came up behind him. "You feel that?"

Stache nodded. "Something's about to crack."

The call came at 0613.

"Unidentified vehicle approaching from north slope. Fast. No response to warnings."

Within seconds, the FOB was alive with movement—boots hitting gravel, weapons being racked, radios flaring. Foster snapped his vest closed and grabbed his kit.

Stache's voice cut clean across the net. "Gun crews mount up. Set overwatch positions. Do not fire unless confirmed hostile."

The truck barreled through the valley floor, mud streaked across the windshield, engine whining in protest. It veered hard just before the first barrier and came to a screeching halt.

A man stumbled out—bleeding, clothes shredded, eyes wide.

"They're coming!" he shouted. "They're right behind me!"

Before he could say more, the first round cracked overhead.

Sniper fire.

Then the sky opened up.

Gunfire rained from the cliffs. It came from both sides—an orchestrated hit. The FOB's outer defenses lit up. Stache was already moving, shouting orders, rallying teams.

"Foster—get to tower three! Jimmy, reinforce south wall. Perez, eyes on that ridge—now!"

The squad snapped into place; each motion a memory rehearsed a hundred times.

Inside the TOC, Lt. Price relayed coordinates to Razor for fire support. "QRF is twenty out. We hold."

Stache grabbed the radio. "We don't hold. We push back."

The fight lasted twenty-six minutes.

But in the moment, it felt like eternity unraveling.

The first sniper shot shattered the comms antenna on tower two, sparks showering down onto the gravel. Before anyone could react, a second round cracked through the outer gate guard shack, narrowly missing Perez as he hit the deck behind a HESCO wall.

"CONTACT NORTH AND EAST! MULTIPLE POSITIONS!" Stache's voice barked through the net, calm but forceful.

Incoming fire cascaded from the ridge—AK bursts, controlled volleys, and RPG fire streaking like firelight across the sky. The first RPG impacted just outside the motor pool, flipping a parked Humvee onto its side. Fuel sprayed across the concrete like a broken artery.

"SMOKE OUT! GUNNERS—SWEEP HIGH!" Stache yelled, sprinting to the control tower. "Johnny, suppress ridge two-zero-five! Foster, get to tower three and grab the Mark 19!"

Foster didn't hesitate. He climbed the ladder as bullets tore through the camo net above him. Dirt and sand erupted around his boots with each impact. He reached the tower, swung the weapon into place, and started thumping grenades in arcs across the tree line.

Below, Perez sprinted through fire to grab spare belts from the ammo tent. Jimmy dropped behind the overturned Humvee, used the wheel well as cover, and opened up with his SAW, sweeping the southern ridge line with heavy bursts.

"WE'VE GOT MOVEMENT NEAR THE CULVERT!" Johnny shouted over the net. "FIVE—NO, SIX HOSTILES—TRYING TO BREACH THE EAST WALL!"

Stache bolted to that side, ducking beneath a barrage of fire. He grabbed two infantry from another squad and flanked right. As he rounded the rear bunker, he caught sight of the silhouettes— black scarves, sand-colored robes, rifles drawn. He didn't wait.

"ENGAGE!"

The next thirty seconds were hell. Rifles cracked; grenades hissed. One of the attackers threw a Molotov, which shattered against the wall but failed to ignite. Stache dropped one insurgent with a tight three-round burst, then another as they tried to leap the barrier.

"WALL IS HOLDING!" Perez called out.

"KEEP THE PRESSURE UP!" Stache responded.

Through the smoke, a drone feed suddenly popped on inside the TOC. Lt. Price shouted into the radio, "Razor is inbound. Two Black Hawks. ETA two minutes. Hold this line!"

Stache keyed his mic. "We're not letting go."

Another RPG launched—this one hitting the edge of tower three. Foster was blown back from the Mark 19, hitting the deck hard. His helmet rolled off, ears ringing.

But he crawled back, bleeding from a cut above his brow, and re-engaged. The ridge shuddered as his next round struck the enemy position, scattering debris and bodies.

"GOOD HIT!" Johnny called out from across the compound, one hand clutching his bleeding arm, the other still on his trigger.

The Black Hawks arrived low and fast. Their miniguns roared, raking the enemy positions with terrifying precision. Dust and fire rose like thunderclouds.

Within seconds, the attackers scattered—some running, others falling.

And just like that, the shooting stopped.

The sky went quiet again.

Except for the sound of boots moving through smoke and the cough of spent weapons cooling in the dust. The wounded man from the truck survived, barely.

At 0645, Razor's air support arrived. Two Black Hawks swept in low, unloading with precision strikes. The ridgeline scattered. The assault broke.

Silence returned—but this time, it was earned.

That night, the squad gathered in the med tent. Johnny's arm was bandaged, his usual sarcasm dulled by blood loss. But he was alive.

Stache stood by the doorway, watching.

Foster sat beside Johnny, quietly praying.

Perez passed out water. "You know," he said, "every time it feels like the end, somehow we're still here."

Foster smiled. "That's because we're not the ones doing the holding."

They all turned to look at him.

He opened his Bible, turned to Psalm 46:1, and read aloud:

"God is our refuge and strength, a very present help in trouble."

Outside, the night wind returned.

The storm had passed.

But so had something else—a sense that they weren't just fighting to survive.

They were fighting with purpose.

And heaven had heard.

Chapter 26: Mourning and Meaning

They spent the next day rebuilding what had been broken.

Tower three was still blackened from the RPG hit. Scorch marks ran down its frame like claw marks left by the valley. Johnny insisted he could still man the turret with one arm—Stache told him to shut up and take the antibiotics.

Perez coordinated replacement parts with Ironhook's supply NCO. Jimmy helped restring the comms wire, high on a ladder, hands shaking from adrenaline that hadn't quite drained.

And Foster? He was back near the wire, shovel in hand, reinforcing sandbags like he was digging the foundation for something sacred.

But not everything could be patched with wire and grit.

They'd lost two.

Private Kellen—killed instantly in the first blast near the southern HESCO.

Sergeant Danvers—bled out during the final exchange, shielding a wounded tech with his own body.

Their names were spoken softly, folded into every conversation like breath.

The squad didn't break. But they felt it.

Jimmy stood longer than usual beside the burn barrel that night, face unreadable. Perez snapped at a wrench that wouldn't budge and walked away before anyone could ask. Foster, usually the first to speak encouragement, sat silent for over an hour, staring at the ridge.

That evening, Captain Smith held a debrief with the entire forward element under the tarp near the TOC. The sunset painted gold across the sandbags.

She didn't stand tall. She stood close.

"We lost two soldiers yesterday," she said. "And we will honor them. But what you did here was nothing short of a miracle."

She turned slowly, making eye contact with each squad.

"Enemy forces executed a coordinated, multi-vector ambush on this base. You stood. You held. You adapted. Every team performed under fire. Every decision saved lives. We lost two... but we saved dozens."

She let the silence hang.

"No one in this valley will forget that. And neither will I."

She stepped back. "You fought well. You lived better. That's victory."

Stache felt the weight in his chest ease—not because the pain had gone—but because the truth had been spoken.

Chaplains from Razor flew in that afternoon. Two of them—one Army, one Afghan. Not to hold service. Just to talk. Sit. Pray.

Stache stood under the shade tarp outside the motor pool when the American chaplain approached.

"Word's traveled," the chaplain said. "They say your men didn't just fight. They held."

Stache nodded once. "We didn't have a choice."

"No," the chaplain replied. "But you had a voice in how you stood."

Foster sat near the fire barrel that evening, flipping his Bible open with the care of someone who finally understood the weight of it.

The Afghan chaplain—gray-bearded, soft-eyed— sat beside him.

"You read from the Injil?" he asked, pointing to the book.

Foster nodded. "Yes, sir."

"You find peace?"

Foster looked up. "More than that. I found a reason."

The chaplain smiled. "Then you will not fall. No matter what comes."

That night, a few villagers from the nearby valley approached the FOB with small bundles—bread, dried herbs, and a goat-skin flask of water. Gifts. Gratitude.

One boy handed Foster a folded cloth— embroidered with two simple words in Pashto: Faith endures.

Foster knelt to eye level, smiled, and whispered, "Yes. It does."

Stache stood atop the same ridge the enemy had once used to rain fire on them.

Now, it was just sky.

He looked out across the valley, the glow of the FOB flickering behind him like a lighthouse in a storm.

His radio buzzed, but he ignored it for a moment.

Hands behind his back, he breathed in the quiet, the smoke, the mercy.

And whispered the words that had carried him farther than bullets ever could:

"Still here, Lord. Still standing."

Chapter 27: Night Watch

Three days later, the mail arrived.

A beat-up convoy rolled in from the main logistics hub, dragging with it two broken trailers, a crushed generator, and five canvas mail bags.

Foster helped offload the bundles while Perez sifted through names.

"Foster, Johnny, Perez—care packages. Jimmy— letter."

Johnny grinned as he tore open a box filled with beef jerky, socks, and a half-melted Snickers bar. "It's the little things, boys."

Foster found a note inside his own: a short letter from his mother, tucked between Bible tracts and a picture he didn't know she still had—him and his brother fishing, years ago, before the uniform, before the weight.

He folded it gently and put it inside his Bible.

Later that evening, Stache called the squad together in the briefing tent. Not for orders—but for rest.

They sat in a circle, gear off, chairs creaking. The air was thick with dust and heat, but their hearts felt a little lighter.

Stache stood at the center.

"I don't have a mission brief for you tonight," he said. "No grid to memorize. No convoy route to prep."

He paused.

"You earned this stillness."

He let the quiet hang.

"When the letters showed up today, it reminded me of something," he continued. "We've all been writing things here. Some in journals. Some in prayers. Some in blood. Someday, someone's gonna read our story. Make sure it's worth passing on."

Perez nodded slowly. Johnny tapped his pen on his boot.

Foster looked down at his Bible, now worn, dog-eared, marked up with verses and names.

"Sir," Foster said, "What about you? What do you write?"

Stache glanced out the flap of the tent, eyes tracing the last light of day.

"Mostly prayers," he said. "Some for protection. Some for forgiveness."

He looked back at them.

"And a few just to say thanks."

That night, the valley was still.

It wasn't the kind of peace that came with certainty. It was the edge-of-your-seat kind—the quiet after the gunfire when everyone listens just a little harder. But it was peace, nonetheless.

Foster sat outside the barracks on an ammo crate, tracing verses in his Bible with his thumb. He wasn't reading—just feeling the shape of the words, the comfort they brought. Jimmy lay nearby with his boots off, tossing a stress ball lazily in the air, eyes half shut but alert. Johnny leaned against the side of the generator shack, humming a tune from a country song no one else knew.

Perez lit a match and stared at the flame before using it to light a cigarette. "Still weird not hearing anything," he said.

"Yeah," Jimmy murmured. "Like the calm before something... or maybe after."

Foster looked up. "It's okay to let it be calm. Even if it's just tonight."

From the watchtower, a soldier laughed at something crackling over the radio. It wasn't loud—but it was real.

Stache walked the perimeter like always, but slower this time. Not scanning for threats. Just walking. Just listening. Boots crunching on gravel, the faint sound of laughter, a chorus of breath not drawn in fear.

Inside the barracks, letters were being written. Some long. Some short. Some just a few lines scribbled across MRE cardboard—I'm okay. Still here. Still believing.

No one said it aloud, but they all felt it.

The war would return.

But tonight, the fight could wait.

And in that stillness, they found something stronger than armor.

Rest.

And the dust—finally—settled.

Chapter 28: Human Error

The morning broke with the kind of light that made everything look clean—even if nothing really was.

Stache stood at the water tank, rinsing off his hands from another maintenance check. Fuel filters, leaking hoses—small things. But they mattered. It gave him control. It gave him something to fix when the rest of the world didn't bend.

Then the call came.

"Command wants a sit-down. Intel gathered from the last assault is leading to a possible retaliatory strike."

Stache nodded, already moving toward the TOC. Perez fell in beside him.

"Think they'll let us lead it?" Perez asked.

Stache didn't answer right away.

"We'll be ready," he said.

Inside the TOC, the air was tense. Captain Smith stood at the projector with overlays pinned to the board. Lt. Price shuffled imagery as two analysts pointed out heat signatures from the drone feed.

"This ridge," Smith said, tapping the map, "was used as a forward scout site. There's a bunker buried here—reinforced, camouflaged. We didn't hit it during the last strike. We think it's the command node for this region."

She looked up. "We're hitting it at dawn. Two squads. One bird for air support. One shot."

Stache spoke low but steady. "Rules of engagement?"

"Standard," Smith replied. "But we're not walking into another ambush. This time, we take the silence away from them."

That night, Stache called the squad together again. But this time, the mood was different. The peace had passed. The edge was back.

They sat outside under low lights, gear in laps, weapons close.

"This next one's not a supply run," Stache said. "It's not a show of force. This is surgical. We find them. We remove them. We don't leave questions."

He looked around.

"But I want to say something before we go. What we're doing matters. But who we are when we do it? That's the part that lasts."

No one spoke, but everyone listened.

Foster looked up. "We leave at dawn?"

Stache nodded. "And we come back. All of us."

The team stood one by one, checking gear, slapping shoulders.

Johnny muttered, "Let's finish what they started."

They launched before first light.

The trucks climbed the narrow switchback trails like metal ghosts. Wind whispered through the scrub brush, the only sound above engines throttling low. The target ridge was twenty minutes out.

Then the lead truck—Johnny's rat rig—hit a soft patch of gravel on a narrow turn.

The vehicle lurched, tires spinning, rear bumper swinging wide over a sharp drop.

"STOP! STOP!" Perez yelled from the second vehicle.

Johnny slammed the brake, overcorrected.

The rear end slipped farther.

"Gun mount! Get out!" Stache ordered, already dismounting.

Jimmy leapt from his position, scrambling up the side with tow cable. Foster moved to flank but slipped on the shale and slid five feet before catching himself.

"Hold that wheel straight, Johnny!" Stache barked, bracing the rear fender with his shoulder.

The whole truck groaned like it was about to roll.

Perez hit the anchor points with the tow line, locked it to truck two. "Winch—go! Now!"

The cable stretched; metal creaked.

And then—traction.

The rat truck jerked back toward center.

Silence followed. Heavy. Breathless.

Johnny climbed out of the driver's seat, pale but grinning. "Well... that was a little close."

No one laughed. Not yet.

But no one had died.

And that was enough.

Back at base that night, Stache sat with the map again, marking where the ridge nearly cost them everything.

He circled it twice.

Then wrote just two words beside it:

Grace held.

Chapter 29: Retaliation

The sun was still below the horizon when the convoy reached staging.

Fog drifted through the low rocks like smoke without fire. The cold bit through uniforms, numbing fingers and making rifle grips feel like ice. Every breath turned to mist.

Stache checked his watch. Zero five twenty-two. Final checks.

The squad moved with quiet precision. Foster secured the comms relay and triple-checked the encryption. Perez finished calibrating the drone uplink, his fingers tapping steadily despite the cold. Jimmy handed out extra ammo belts, one by one, each motion practiced, automatic. Johnny, riding rear security this time, slid into the turret like he was climbing back into a memory.

"Stay sharp," Stache said. "We hit hard. We hit fast. No freelancing. Stick to your roles, watch each other's backs."

Lt. Price moved alongside them, his kit tighter than usual, the edges of nervousness visible in the set of his jaw. It was his first strike with Stache's team. He didn't speak—just nodded when spoken to, clutching his rifle a little too hard.

Overwatch called in.

"Eyes on the ridge. No movement. Target bunker location verified."

Captain Smith's voice crackled across the channel. "Execute on green. You're cleared."

Green light flicked.

They moved like a fist through the valley— controlled, deliberate, silent.

The lead team flanked right across the rocky incline, taking overwatch positions like shadows on the high ground. Stache's element cut straight in, low to the terrain, staggered, sweeping their sectors as they moved.

As they neared the objective, the world narrowed to heartbeats and footfalls. The bunker crouched against the cliffside like a buried serpent. Its silence felt more dangerous than any known threat.

Foster reached the first marker. "Movement— doorway left side, two shadows."

Stache raised his fist. The squad froze.

Perez pulled the pin on a flashbang, lobbed it over the ledge.

Crack.

Screams. Footsteps. A burst of gunfire from the entrance.

Three hostiles rushed out in a disorganized panic, blinded. Jimmy and Foster engaged immediately, controlled bursts dropping two. The third scrambled back, spraying wildly before disappearing into the shadows.

"Advance! Breach pattern—move!" Stache barked.

They stacked tight, cleared the threshold with brutal clarity. The first room erupted in dust and shouting. Each member knew their job. Johnny secured the rear. Perez cut the corner left. Jimmy and Foster took center.

Stache moved forward, scanning and issuing commands with clipped efficiency.

In the command chamber, red light blinked from damaged electronics. Maps and comm logs scattered. The scent of diesel and sweat lingered.

Then—movement.

From a shadowed alcove, a man lunged.

Blade drawn.

Lt. Price froze.

Just for a second. One heartbeat too long.

The blade flashed.

Stache was faster.

He intercepted the man mid-stride, weapon raised. Two clean shots, chest and shoulder. The man dropped, crumpling into the dust.

Lt. Price's breath shook. He backed against the wall, rifle clutched uselessly.

Stache stood over the body, breathing steady. He looked at Price—not in anger, but with the weight of a thousand near-misses.

"You're here," he said. "You made it. That's what counts. Learn from it."

Price nodded, shame twisting his features—but somewhere behind it, respect took root.

They cleared the last corridor.

Seven hostiles down. No friendlies lost. The bunker was neutralized.

Outside, the Black Hawk circled once before banking west. Extraction was already inbound.

Stache walked the ridge line alone, the same one once used to watch their every move. Now it belonged to them.

He paused at the edge, looked out over the valley, and let himself feel it—not pride. Not revenge.

Relief. Redemption.

Lt. Price approached slowly, still pale.

"I should've moved," he said quietly.

"You will next time," Stache replied. "Fear's a teacher. Learn the lesson."

Perez stepped past, brushing dust from his sleeves like it was just another day. "We came. We saw. We rebuilt the ridge."

Foster stood in the center of the ridge, hands on his hips, breath steady, posture calm. He whispered a word—just one.

"Victory."

And for the first time, it wasn't a word meant to justify blood.

It was a word meant to honor grace.

The silence wasn't theirs anymore.

Now, it was earned.

Chapter 30: The Edge of Home

They came home to quiet.

Not silence—but the kind of quiet that meant something had shifted. The kind of quiet that let you hear your own heartbeat again. The FOB had resumed its routines—vehicles moving, generators humming, soldiers walking—but everyone moved with a different weight. Like the ridge strike had pressed something into the earth that wouldn't come back up.

The mission had ended, but the echo of it followed each step.

Word spread fast: reinforcement units were inbound. In four days, the rotation would change. Fresh boots would hit the wire, and their time here would be done. Just a few more patrols. Just a few more nights.

Stache stepped down from the truck last. He didn't say a word. Just patted Johnny on the shoulder and walked straight to the motor pool. Not because anything was broken—because it was familiar. Routine. Tangible. A way to hold on just a little longer.

Foster lingered behind, his helmet tucked under his arm, eyes scanning the horizon like it might speak again. He felt lighter, but not because the danger was gone. Because the mission had meant something.

"Hey," Jimmy said, pulling up beside him, "You pray again after that?"

Foster nodded. "Yeah. Not just for us. For them too."

Jimmy raised a brow but said nothing. He didn't need to.

Later that night, Captain Smith gathered the key leaders in the TOC. It wasn't a celebration. It was a marker.

"You did what few can," she said. "You took ground and gave nothing back. You neutralized a threat without losing a single man. That doesn't happen. And it wasn't luck. It was discipline, leadership, and faith—in each other and something more."

She let the silence settle.

"Now I need you to do the harder thing—come down. Reintegrate. Let your guard down a little. You're not machines. You're men. And I want you home the same way you came into this valley— alive. Whole. Ready to live again."

No one spoke. They didn't need to. They understood what wasn't being said: the hardest part wasn't surviving the firefights—it was learning how to stop bracing for the next one.

That evening, the squad gathered again—this time around the fire barrel not out of stress, but because it had become home. Familiar. Sacred.

Johnny passed around packets of powdered hot cocoa someone's wife had mailed. Perez shared a few stale cookies from a crushed box. Jimmy tuned a radio and found a station playing something close to jazz. It didn't matter what it was. It was music.

They talked more than usual. Not just about the mission—but about home. About movies they missed. Food. Girls. Family. Johnny talked about rebuilding his dad's old motorcycle. Jimmy said he might go back to school. Even Perez, ever the cynic, admitted he was thinking of getting baptized—"just in case," he said with a crooked grin.

Foster took out his notebook. Wrote a new line.

Some victories don't make headlines. But they echo.

He passed it to Stache, who read it, then folded the paper and tucked it into his breast pocket.

"We're not done," Stache said. "But we're standing."

Perez grinned. "And next time, Johnny doesn't drive."

Johnny rolled his eyes. "One close call and suddenly I'm a legend."

They laughed.

And the fire cracked like it agreed.

Above them, stars returned to a sky that had once rained fire.

Now, it simply watched.

They were still there.

And tomorrow—when the dust stirred again—they would be too.

Chapter 31: The Handoff

The sun rose flat and red over the valley, painting the rocks in rust.

It was a different kind of morning. One marked not by adrenaline, but reflection. The last patrol was today. One final loop through the Echo corridor before the new squad took over. A final drive to say goodbye—not just to the terrain, but to who they had been when they first arrived.

Stache stood outside the barracks before first light, watching the dust lift in thin spirals. He didn't feel nervous. He didn't feel ready either. He just felt present.

Foster stepped beside him, sipping from a canteen. "Feels weird," he said.

"What does?"

"Knowing this one's the last. Like we're closing a chapter, but the pages are still warm."

Stache nodded. "It's supposed to feel that way. Means we made it mean something."

The squad rolled out slow and steady.

No chatter. No music. Just the hum of engines and the occasional burst of static. They hit every checkpoint, waved to every ANA post, nodded at every farmer in the fields. Every click felt like it carried memories strapped to the axle.

Near Ridge 205—the place where everything had changed—they stopped.

They dismounted, quiet. Foster ran a hand along the edge of the same rock he'd used for cover weeks ago. Johnny sat on the hood of the lead Humvee, eyes on the ridgeline.

Perez lit a cigarette and offered one to Jimmy. Jimmy shook his head but smiled.

Stache crouched near the edge, pulled out the folded line Foster had written.

Some victories don't make headlines. But they echo.

He tore off a corner, wrote today's date, and tucked it under a small pile of stones.

A marker. Not for others. For them.

On the drive back, they passed a new convoy coming in—fresh faces, clean uniforms, uncertain eyes.

One of the new soldiers gave a sharp wave. Foster returned it.

"They don't know yet," he said.

Stache answered without looking. "They will."

Back at the FOB, the transition began.

Half the squad was pulled for rest and admin, the other half assigned to shadow the incoming unit.

Their job: pass the torch. Teach them the ridgelines, the soft curves of the road that seemed safe but weren't, the way the dust moved when trouble was coming.

Johnny took point leading the new gunner through the fire barrel story—where they laughed, where they bled, where they learned.

Jimmy rode lead for two new NCOs, narrating the terrain like a tour guide who'd lived the route rather than studied it.

Foster walked beside a wide-eyed private, pointing out how the valley breathed differently depending on the time of day. "This isn't just dirt," he said. "It's memory. Respect it."

Gear started coming off.

One vest at a time. One rifle. One last nod to the armor that had held more than bullets.

Stache kept his dog tags. And the verse. Isaiah 41:10, still folded in the flap of his vest.

Perez dropped a single shell casing on the barracks step. "Souvenir," he said with a grin.

The rest of the squad laughed.

Foster held back for a moment, looking out over the valley.

He whispered one more prayer.

Not for protection.

But for peace.

And this time, he wasn't the only one praying.

Chapter 32: Homebound Reflections

The next three days blurred between briefings, gear inventories, and moments that felt like the last page of a book you weren't quite ready to finish.

Reinforcements had settled in. Their routines were beginning to mirror the old squad's. Schedules were set. Guard posts rotated. Convoys launched with new voices on the net. But echoes of the outgoing team lingered in every corner of the FOB.

In the motor pool, grease stains bore initials scratched into the floor. At the chapel tent, someone had pinned a Psalm to the bulletin board in Foster's handwriting.

He will cover you with His feathers, and under His wings you will find refuge... — Psalm 91:4

Some things stayed. Some things had to.

The transition wasn't just technical—it was emotional. Every file handed over came with a story. Every route marker came with a warning. The incoming soldiers, wide-eyed at first, began to ask questions not found on any map.

"Where's the best cover if it pops off at checkpoint six?"

"What's the telltale sound the ridge makes before wind shifts?"

"Where did Danvers fall?"

The old squad didn't shy away. They answered with honesty, sometimes with a chuckle, sometimes with silence. It wasn't just information—it was inheritance.

Stache spent the final handoff morning walking the wire alone. He didn't bring a radio. He didn't need it. He knew this ground by heart. Every foot of gravel, every breath of wind, every shadow line.

He met the new platoon sergeant halfway through the loop. Sergeant Kline. Solid. Young, but steady.

"You all set?" Stache asked.

Kline nodded. "We've got the files, the routes, the map overlays. Your guys have been more than helpful."

"You don't have to do it the way we did," Stache said. "But know that everything in this valley costs something. Pay attention."

Kline didn't smile. He just nodded. That was enough.

That night, the squad shared their final fire.

It wasn't loud. There were no speeches. Just warm cocoa, a few quiet stories, and a sense of something sacred closing.

Stache stood as the flames danced low, then moved slowly around the circle, stopping by each man.

"Johnny," he said, "what's the first thing you're doing back stateside?"

Johnny smirked. "I'm eating three full racks of ribs, sleeping for two days, and then rebuilding that motorcycle with my dad."

Everyone chuckled. Stache moved on.

"Perez?"

Perez leaned back; cigarette tucked behind his ear. "I'm taking my mom to church. She made me promise I'd go with her. Maybe I'll keep going."

Jimmy nodded beside him. "I'm gonna enroll. Get my degree. Stop putting it off."

Foster looked up from his notebook. "Honestly? I just want to sit on my porch with my Bible, a cold drink, and not hear a single helicopter for a month."

They all smiled at that.

Before the fire died out, Stache stood again and cleared his throat. "Also—word from battalion. You've all racked up more than enough leave time during this deployment. When we get home, you're officially off duty for a full thirty days. No formations, no alerts, no last-minute nonsense. Just rest."

The squad let out a collective exhale. A few clapped. Jimmy fist-bumped Johnny.

Stache held up a finger. "That said—don't go getting soft. Army standards still apply when we get back. I don't want to see any busted tape tests or someone crying during a two-mile run."

Laughter rippled around the fire.

Then he walked to his seat, and when it came to Stache, no one asked. But he answered anyway.

"I'm going home," he said. "To my wife. To the little house she fixed up while I was gone. I'm gonna take off this vest, and I'm not putting it back on for a long time."

A quiet settled then—not heavy, but full. Like a chapter written well enough to let it end.

Johnny handed off his last rounds to the new gunner with a pat on the shoulder. "Keep her warm, and don't flinch at the first pop."

Jimmy left a photo of their squad pinned to the back of the main comms desk.

Perez scratched his name into the corner of the mess tent frame. "Tradition."

Foster offered a spare pocket Bible to the private who had shadowed him. "You'll need this more than a rifle on some days."

And Stache? He sat quietly, watching his men. He didn't need to say much.

They'd already said it all—through sacrifice, through service, through standing.

When the fire dimmed to embers, they stayed a little longer. Just enough to let it burn into memory.

Tomorrow, they'd board the flight home.

But tonight, they were still here.

Together.

Chapter 33: Return and Reunion

The morning of departure came with no fanfare.

The sky was pale and open. No helicopters overhead. No gunfire in the distance. Just the soft hum of generators and the occasional scuff of boots on gravel.

Bags were packed. Weapons cleared. Armor turned in.

The squad stood on the tarmac in a quiet line, duffels at their feet, watching as the transport plane's engines warmed.

Foster wore his notebook in his chest pocket, like a shield made of ink and hope. Jimmy had headphones in, playing music no one else could hear. Johnny held nothing—just his hands in his pockets and a look in his eyes that said he wasn't ready to miss this place, but he knew he would.

Stache moved between them, stopping just long enough to make eye contact. No words. Just presence.

When the ramp lowered, the sound broke the silence like thunder breaking cloud.

They boarded without ceremony.

Inside, the cabin was cold and loud.

No one spoke. Some slept. Others stared at nothing.

Foster wrote something in his notebook and tore the page. He passed it to Stache as the wheels lifted off the ground.

"Thank you for showing us how to fight the right battles."

Stache folded the note and placed it in his pocket beside Isaiah 41:10.

Outside the window, the ridgeline shrank beneath the clouds.

They didn't leave it behind. They carried it with them.

Hours later, the wheels touched down back on American soil.

Families waited beyond the gates. Flags waved. Sunlight hit differently.

They stepped off the plane as a unit one last time.

No longer in formation.

But never out of step.

Home.

The parking lot outside the hangar buzzed with reunions. Kids running. Flags waving. Cries that started as laughter. But Stache stood still for a moment longer, just watching it all.

Then he saw her.

Emily.

Hair pulled back, eyes scanning until they found his. No makeup. No signs. Just her—real, waiting, steady.

He didn't run. He walked.

And when she reached him, she didn't cry. She just wrapped her arms around him and held on like the world had stopped spinning for a second.

"You're home," she whispered.

Stache nodded into her shoulder. "We made it."

She pulled back just enough to look him in the eyes. "Did you leave it all there?"

"No," he said, a small smile tugging his mouth. "I brought back what mattered."

They walked together toward the car, her hand in his, and for the first time in months, his steps felt light.

Not because the weight was gone.

But because he wasn't carrying it alone anymore.

Later that evening, after the noise of the crowd had faded and the bags were inside, they sat on the back porch of their small house. The breeze rustled the trees gently. The world felt wide again.

Emily poured herself a cup of coffee while Stache cracked open a cold Purple Haze Bang energy drink—ice cold, pulled straight from the fridge where she'd stocked an entire case just for him. She knew him well, and he'd joked for years that he survived Army mornings on caffeine and faith. The first sip hit like a rush of home.

They sat together on the back porch of their small house, her hand in his as they rocked side by side.

"You look different," she said softly.

Stache nodded. "I feel different. Not broken—just... reshaped."

She turned to him. "I prayed for that. For years. I always hoped the Lord would work something deep in you—not just bring you home safe, but bring you home whole."

Stache looked down at his cup. "He did. And He used the valley to do it."

Emily's eyes welled up, but she held them back. "Tell me."

So he did.

He told her about the night Foster gave his life to Christ. About the verse that kept him grounded—Isaiah 41:10. About the chaplain with the quiet eyes who reminded him it was okay to not carry it all. About how prayer turned from a habit into a lifeline. About the fire barrel, the laughter, the fear, the victory. About how every single day out there, he tried to walk with God—not perfectly, but deliberately.

"I didn't come home the same," he said finally. "I came home walking closer than I ever have before. And not just because I needed Him—but because I wanted Him."

Emily leaned her head on his shoulder. "That's all I ever prayed for."

They sat like that for a long while—just holding hands and thanking the One who had never let go of either of them.

Home wasn't just a place.

It was a promise kept.

Epilogue: What Waits Beneath

Six weeks later.

The rhythms of home had settled around Stache like an old, familiar coat—soft, worn, grounding. Church on Sundays. Coffee (for her), Bang (for him). Mornings on the porch. Life was quieter. Gentler. He kept his promise to Emily and hadn't put on a uniform since stepping off that flight.

But some habits die slow.

He still walked the perimeter of their small backyard every night. Still checked locks. Still watched the treeline at dusk, even if it was just a stand of pines outside their fence.

Then one night—something changed.

He found a package on the front step. No postage. No return address. Just his name—stamped in black ink across the top.

Inside was a small, dusty notebook.

A name was scrawled across the inside cover.

Danvers.

Stache's blood ran cold. Danvers had died in the valley. He'd seen it. Buried him. Prayed over him.

He flipped through the pages—sketches, coordinates, hand-drawn maps, and one phrase written over and over again:

"They're not done yet."

The final page held one line in handwriting that wasn't Danvers':

You thought it was over. But the silence was just the start.

Stache stood there in the fading light, the world narrowing around him.

Emily stepped out onto the porch. "Everything okay?"

Stache looked up, the notebook closed tight in his hand.

He smiled gently. "Yeah. Just some old dust."

But in his gut, he knew:

Something had followed them home.

And this fight wasn't finished.

To be continued...

30-Day Devotional Challenge

Day 1: The Right Battles

Scripture:

1 Samuel 17:45–47 (ESV)

"But David said to the Philistine, 'You come to me with a sword and with a spear and with a javelin, but I come to you in the name of the Lord of hosts, the God of the armies of Israel, whom you have defied. This day the Lord will deliver you into my hand... For the battle is the Lord's, and He will give you into our hand.'"

Devotion:

In *Finding God in the Mountains of Afghanistan*, Stache and his squad faced overwhelming odds—ambushes, mortar fire, and decisions that determined life or death. But just like David before Goliath, they weren't alone. Stache didn't just rely on tactics and muscle—he leaned on Scripture, prayer, and the belief that God was walking with them through every valley.

David's bold faith reminds us that victory doesn't come from the size of your weapon, but the size of your God. When fear looms like a giant, remember: God has already won the battle. Your job is to stand in faith and show up.

Whether you're in uniform or navigating life's civilian struggles, your giants are real—fear, trauma, temptation, insecurity. But so is your Savior.

Reflection Questions:

What giants are you currently facing in life or service?

In what ways can you trust God to fight those battles for you?

How can you step forward today with David-like courage and faith?

Challenge:

Write down one "giant" in your life on a piece of paper. Then, speak 1 Samuel 17:47 aloud over it. Pray, surrender it to God, and trust Him to deliver you.

Day 2: Obedient Steps That Break Walls

Scripture:

Joshua 6:2–5 (ESV)

"And the Lord said to Joshua, 'See, I have given Jericho into your hand, with its king and mighty men of valor... On the seventh day you shall march around the city seven times... and the wall of the city will fall down flat.'"

Devotion:

In the story of Joshua, God gave a battle plan that defied logic. No battering rams. No surprise attack. Just marching, trumpets, and obedience. And yet, victory came—not because of might, but because of trust.

In *Finding God in the Mountains of Afghanistan*, Stache led his squad on convoys through danger zones, trusting God not just for safety but for direction. Sometimes, the hardest part wasn't the firefight—it was following God's leading even when it didn't make sense.

Jericho's story is a reminder: God's methods may not always align with human strategies, but obedience to Him always leads to breakthrough. What looks like a wall today may be ready to fall if you'll trust and walk.

Reflection Questions:

Are you trying to knock down walls in your life using your own strength?

What is God asking you to do—even if it seems unconventional?

How can you practice consistent obedience, even when you don't see immediate results?

Challenge:

Identify one area where you've been pushing in your own strength. Pause. Ask God what His "marching orders" are. Then write them down and commit to following them for the next seven days.

Sometimes victory begins with walking in quiet obedience. March on.

Day 3: Strength in Small Numbers

Scripture:

Judges 7:7 (ESV)

"And the Lord said to Gideon, 'With the 300 men who lapped I will save you and give the Midianites into your hand.'"

Devotion:

Gideon didn't start with an elite force—he started with fear and doubt. God cut his army from thousands down to just 300. Why? So that when the victory came, everyone would know it was God who delivered, not human strength.

In *Finding God in the Mountains of Afghanistan*, Stache's squad often felt outnumbered—low visibility, limited backup, high stress. But time and again, it wasn't their numbers or firepower that carried them through. It was their unity, their faith, and the God who never left their side.

Like Gideon, you may be feeling outgunned, under-equipped, or unworthy. But God specializes in using the unlikely. He's not asking for your strength—He's asking for your surrender.

Reflection Questions:

When have you felt overwhelmed by the size of the battle in front of you?

How has God shown up in your life through unlikely means or small moments?

How can you lead with courage and humility, knowing victory comes from Him?

Challenge:

Write down one area where you feel insufficient or outnumbered. Now write a prayer asking God to use your weakness for His glory—just like He did with Gideon's 300.

God doesn't need numbers. He just needs your "yes."

Day 4: Bold Faith, Quiet Strength

Scripture:

1 Samuel 14:6 (ESV)

"Jonathan said to the young man who carried his armor, 'Come, let us go over to the garrison of these uncircumcised. It may be that the Lord will work for us, for nothing can hinder the Lord from saving by many or by few.'"

Devotion:

Jonathan didn't wait for orders. He trusted that if God was in it, victory was possible. His courage wasn't loud—it was grounded. And his armor-bearer? He followed without hesitation, believing in the mission and the man beside him.

In *Finding God in the Mountains of Afghanistan*, there were moments when bold steps had to be taken—when waiting meant danger and faith required movement. Whether it was stepping forward during an ambush or helping lead during uncertainty, Stache and his men had to believe that God could move through a few faithful hearts.

Your courage may not always look like a battlefield charge. Sometimes it looks like a quiet decision to lead, to pray, or to speak when others stay silent. Faith moves mountains—but it often begins with one obedient step.

Reflection Questions:

What decision is God calling you to make that requires bold faith?

How can you be like Jonathan—or his armor-bearer—by trusting God and supporting those beside you?

Who can you encourage today to take a step of faith?

Challenge:

Pray and ask God to reveal one area where you need to act instead of wait. Then take a small but deliberate step in faith today—just like Jonathan did.

Sometimes the first step of courage is just saying, "Let's go."

Day 5: Authority and Faith

Scripture:

Matthew 8:8–10 (ESV)

"But the centurion replied, 'Lord, I am not worthy to have you come under my roof, but only say the word, and my servant will be healed. For I too am a man under authority, with soldiers under me...' When Jesus heard this, he marveled and said, 'Truly, I tell you, with no one in Israel have I found such faith.'"

Devotion:

The centurion knew what it meant to lead, to follow, and to trust orders. But he also knew Jesus had authority that surpassed any rank. His faith didn't require signs—just a word from the One who commanded creation.

In *Finding God in the Mountains of Afghanistan*, Stache lived in a world of rank, routine, and risk. But over time, he learned that true authority wasn't in stripes or stars—it was in surrender to the King who led from the front lines of every spiritual battle.

Like the centurion, we're called to trust that God doesn't need to "show up" the way we expect. His word is enough. His presence is sure. And His authority—over fear, sickness, sin, and death—is final.

Reflection Questions:

Where in your life do you need to trust God's authority more fully?

How does the centurion's faith challenge your understanding of leadership and humility?

Who around you needs to see that kind of faith in action today?

Challenge:

Think about an area where you've been waiting for God to "show up." Speak His promises over it instead. Declare, "Lord, only say the word," and trust that He already has.

Real authority starts with faith that submits to the One in command.

Day 6: Fire from Heaven, Faith on the Ground

Scripture:

1 Kings 18:36–39 (ESV)

"Elijah the prophet came near and said, 'O Lord, God of Abraham, Isaac, and Israel, let it be known this day that you are God in Israel... Answer me, O Lord, answer me, that this people may know that you, O Lord, are God...' Then the fire of the Lord fell... and when all the people saw it, they fell on their faces and said, 'The Lord, he is God; the Lord, he is God.'"

Devotion:

Elijah didn't fight with weapons—he fought with faith. Surrounded by hundreds of false prophets, he stood alone, called on the Lord, and watched fire fall from heaven. His confidence wasn't in the spectacle—it was in knowing Who sent the fire.

In *Finding God in the Mountains of Afghanistan*, there were moments when the only answer was prayer. No backup. No perfect plan. Just the choice to believe God still shows up when His people call on Him with bold faith.

You may never face prophets of Baal or call down fire, but you will face opposition—on base, in your heart, in life. Like Elijah, your greatest weapon is your unwavering trust in God. Sometimes, the fire doesn't fall until the prayer is bold enough to ask for it.

Reflection Questions:

Where do you need to take a bold stand for your faith today?

How has God proven Himself faithful to you when you've trusted Him in difficult circumstances?

What would it look like for you to pray with Elijah-like boldness?

Challenge:

Spend 10 minutes in bold, unfiltered prayer today. Don't ask small—ask heaven-sized. Write down your request and wait expectantly. God answers faith.

The fire falls where bold faith stands.

Day 7: Resilient in the Firefight

Scripture:

2 Corinthians 11:24–27 (ESV)

"Five times I received at the hands of the Jews the forty lashes less one. Three times I was beaten with rods. Once I was stoned. Three times I was shipwrecked... in danger from rivers, danger from robbers, danger from my own people... in toil and hardship, through many a sleepless night..."

Devotion:

Paul didn't sugarcoat suffering. He walked through it—over and over again—and kept pressing forward. His endurance wasn't fueled by pride, but by purpose. His mission mattered more than his comfort.

In *Finding God in the Mountains of Afghanistan*, Stache's squad endured more than physical hardship. Sleep deprivation, fear, loss, and mental exhaustion weighed on them—but they kept going. Not because it was easy, but because the mission was bigger than the moment.

Maybe you're battle-worn too. Maybe your suffering isn't visible, but internal—grief, shame, burnout. Paul reminds us: endurance is not weakness. It's proof of faith under fire. God doesn't just carry you through—He refines you in the fire.

Reflection Questions:

What hardships have tested your faith or perseverance recently?

How has God carried you through seasons when you felt like quitting?

What's one way you can encourage someone else to keep pressing on today?

Challenge:

Write a short letter or message to someone you know who's struggling. Remind them of Paul's endurance—and that they're not alone in their fight.

Resilience isn't about how strong you are—it's about who strengthens you.

Day 8: Peace in the Chaos

Scripture:

Mark 4:39–41 (ESV)

"And he awoke and rebuked the wind and said to the sea, 'Peace! Be still!' And the wind ceased, and there was a great calm. He said to them, 'Why are you so afraid? Have you still no faith?' And they were filled with great fear and said to one another, 'Who then is this, that even the wind and the sea obey him?'"

Devotion:

Storms don't just hit the sea—they hit the soul. In the middle of a howling windstorm, the disciples forgot who was in the boat with them. Fear overtook faith—until Jesus spoke.

In *Finding God in the Mountains of Afghanistan*, Stache's squad often moved through literal and spiritual storms. Whether under fire or under pressure, peace didn't come from the absence of conflict—but from remembering who held command.

You might be walking through a storm right now—family troubles, financial strain, spiritual confusion. Don't miss this: Jesus never promised storm-free living. But He did promise His presence in the boat.

Reflection Questions:

What personal "storm" are you currently facing?

In what ways is Jesus calling you to trust His presence, even when you don't feel calm?

How can you bring peace to others today by pointing them to the One who still calms storms?

Challenge:

Take five minutes in silence today. Picture yourself in the boat with Jesus during your storm. Ask Him to speak, "Peace, be still," over your heart—and believe that He will.

When Christ is in your boat, no storm has the final word.

Day 9: Battle-Ready

Scripture:

Ephesians 6:10–18 (ESV)

"Finally, be strong in the Lord and in the strength of his might. Put on the whole armor of God... that you may be able to withstand in the evil day, and having done all, to stand firm."

Devotion:

Paul doesn't tell us to charge without armor—he tells us to suit up in the strength of the Lord. Every day is a battle. Not just against bullets or enemies, but against fear, temptation, depression, and spiritual attack.

In *Finding God in the Mountains of Afghanistan*, Stache's squad geared up before every convoy—helmets, vests, comms, weapons. But what truly protected them wasn't only what they wore—it was the prayer, the unity, and the Word spoken before boots even hit gravel.

The armor of God is your daily kit: truth, righteousness, peace, faith, salvation, and the Word. Without it, you're vulnerable. With it, you're ready—not just to survive, but to stand.

Reflection Questions:

Which piece of God's armor do you need to strengthen most right now?

How are you preparing spiritually each day before stepping into battle—whether literal or personal?

How can you help a brother or sister in Christ get battle-ready?

Challenge:

Write down each piece of the armor of God on a notecard or journal page. Each morning this week, declare them over yourself as you prepare for the day—like spiritual PT.

Don't just wear armor. Stand in it.

Day 10: The Shepherd Who Stays

Scripture:

John 10:11–15 (ESV)

"I am the good shepherd. The good shepherd lays down his life for the sheep… I know my own and my own know me… and I lay down my life for the sheep."

Devotion:

A hired hand runs when danger comes. But a good shepherd stays.

Jesus doesn't just call Himself a shepherd—He proves it by laying down His life for us. He knows you by name. He leads with love. He protects with power.

In *Finding God in the Mountains of Afghanistan*, leadership wasn't just about giving orders—it was about showing up, standing in the gap, and making sure no one got left behind. Stache earned his men's trust by doing just that—by being the kind of leader who didn't abandon his squad when things got hard.

Jesus is that leader for you. You may feel overlooked or vulnerable, but the Good Shepherd never clocks out. He sees you. He knows you. And He never leaves.

Reflection Questions:

How does Jesus' role as your Good Shepherd give you comfort and courage?

In what ways can you lead others with the same sacrificial care?

Who in your life needs to be reminded that they're not forgotten by God?

Challenge:

Reach out to someone today who may feel isolated—whether in your squad, unit, workplace, or family. Remind them they are seen, known, and loved.

The Good Shepherd never leaves the field.

Day 11: Unshakable in the Fire

Scripture:

Daniel 3:16–18 (ESV)

"Shadrach, Meshach, and Abednego answered and said to the king... 'Our God whom we serve is able to deliver us... But if not, be it known to you... that we will not serve your gods or worship the golden image.'"

Devotion:

Courage isn't always about charging in—it's often about standing firm when everyone else backs down. These three men didn't just believe God could save them—they were willing to burn even if He didn't.

In *Finding God in the Mountains of Afghanistan*, not every moment came with a guarantee of deliverance. But what defined Stache's squad wasn't their gear or their tactics—it was the unshakable resolve to do what was right, even under fire.

Faith isn't measured by outcomes—it's measured by trust. The kind of trust that says, "Even if God doesn't change this... I'll still stand."

Reflection Questions:

Where are you being called to stand firm in your faith today?

How can you trust God's goodness, even when outcomes are uncertain?

Who's watching your example and being strengthened by your courage?

Challenge:

Write "But if not..." on a sticky note or in your journal. Let it remind you that your faith isn't conditional. Stand tall—even in the fire.

Real faith doesn't flinch at the furnace.

Day 12: When God Parts the Impossible

Scripture:

Exodus 14:13–14 (ESV)

"And Moses said to the people, 'Fear not, stand firm, and see the salvation of the Lord… The Lord will fight for you, and you have only to be silent.'"

Devotion:

The Red Sea wasn't just a body of water—it was a wall of fear, a symbol of helplessness. Trapped between an army and an ocean, Moses didn't panic. He trusted. And God didn't just make a way—He made history.

In *Finding God in the Mountains of Afghanistan*, there were missions where backup wasn't coming, and options were slim. Yet, Stache and his squad saw God show up—sometimes not before the tension, but always in time. That's what faith does. It stands firm in front of the impossible and waits on God to move.

You may feel cornered right now, pressed on all sides. But don't flinch. Stand firm. God hasn't forgotten how to part seas.

Reflection Questions:

What feels "impossible" in your life right now?

How is God asking you to stand still and trust instead of striving?

Who in your circle needs a reminder that God is still a Way maker?

Challenge:

Make a list of the "Red Sea" moments in your past where God came through. Let it be your testimony today—evidence that He parts waters.

When you can't move forward, faith stands still—and watches God do the impossible.

Day 13: Healing in Humility

Scripture:

2 Kings 5:10–14 (ESV)

"And Elisha sent a messenger to him, saying, 'Go and wash in the Jordan seven times… and you shall be clean.' But Naaman was angry… So he turned and went away in a rage… So he went down and dipped himself… and his flesh was restored."

Devotion:

Naaman expected healing to come in grand, dignified ways. Instead, God used something simple—obedience through muddy water. It wasn't until Naaman humbled himself that the miracle came.

In *Finding God in the Mountains of Afghanistan*, Stache and his men learned that strength wasn't always about firepower—it was about submission to something greater. Real healing often came through vulnerability, through quiet acts of prayer, through laying pride down at the feet of grace.

What are you holding onto that might be blocking your healing or breakthrough? Pride? Control? Anger? Sometimes, the command is simple: "Wash and be clean."

Reflection Questions:

Is there something in your life God is asking you to surrender in humility?

How can you respond with obedience—even when it doesn't look how you expected?

What would "washing in the Jordan" look like in your situation?

Challenge:

Pray and ask God to reveal any pride, resentment, or fear holding you back. Write it down. Then surrender it to Him in prayer—and walk forward clean.

The path to healing begins with a humble step into the water.

Day 14: Eyes on Jesus

Scripture:

Matthew 14:28–31 (ESV)

"And Peter answered him, 'Lord, if it is you, command me to come to you on the water.' He said, 'Come.' So Peter got out of the boat and walked on the water… But when he saw the wind, he was afraid, and beginning to sink he cried out, 'Lord, save me.' Jesus immediately reached out his hand and took hold of him…"

Devotion:

Peter's story reminds us: faith doesn't mean fear is gone—it means we move forward anyway. He walked on water because his eyes were fixed on Jesus. The moment he shifted his gaze to the storm, he sank.

In *Finding God in the Mountains of Afghanistan*, the storms came fast—IED threats, loss, fatigue. But when Stache or his squad kept their eyes on the mission God had for them—and not the chaos—they stood firm. They advanced. Even when they stumbled, God reached out.

Life's storms can distract and overwhelm. But Jesus still calls: "Come." Step out. Trust. Keep your eyes on Him—not the waves.

Reflection Questions:

What storms in your life are pulling your attention away from Jesus?

How can you re-center your focus today?

What step of faith is Jesus asking you to take, even if the waters seem rough?

Challenge:

Take 10 minutes today to unplug from distractions and focus on Jesus. Pray, worship, or sit in silence. Refix your gaze on the One who calms the storm.

Faith keeps walking when fear says sink.

Day 15: A Reach of Faith

Scripture:

Mark 5:27–29 (ESV)

"She had heard the reports about Jesus and came up behind him in the crowd and touched his garment. For she said, 'If I touch even his garments, I will be made well.' And immediately the flow of blood dried up, and she felt in her body that she was healed of her disease."

Devotion:

Twelve years of suffering didn't stop her. Shame didn't stop her. A crowd didn't stop her. The woman with the issue of blood had one goal—Jesus. And with one desperate reach, everything changed.

In *Finding God in the Mountains of Afghanistan*, healing didn't always look like recovery—it looked like reaching. Reaching for peace. Reaching for purpose. Reaching for God in the middle of trauma. When Stache and his squad reached out—even in weakness—God met them with strength.

Maybe you feel worn out, pushed to the edge. But there's power in the reach. No ceremony required. Just faith.

Reflection Questions:

What pain or struggle have you been carrying alone?

Are you willing to reach through the "crowd" and trust Jesus with it?

What would healing look like if you placed that burden in His hands?

Challenge:

Write a simple prayer today that says, "Jesus, I'm reaching." Then picture placing your burden in His hands—and leave it there.

One reach of faith is stronger than a thousand steps of doubt.

Day 16: The Power to Change

Scripture:

Acts 9:3–6 (ESV)

"Now as he went on his way, he approached Damascus, and suddenly a light from heaven shone around him. And falling to the ground, he heard a voice saying to him, 'Saul, Saul, why are you persecuting me?'... 'I am Jesus, whom you are persecuting. But rise and enter the city, and you will be told what you are to do.'"

Devotion:

Saul wasn't searching for Jesus—Jesus found him. In one moment of light, a persecutor became a preacher. A hardened man became a vessel of grace. God didn't just forgive Saul—He repurposed him.

In *Finding God in the Mountains of Afghanistan*, Foster's transformation echoes Saul's. Hardened by routine and scars, he wasn't seeking a spiritual awakening. But grace found him—through conversation, compassion, and conviction. He rose from darkness with new direction.

Maybe you think you've gone too far. Maybe someone you love seems beyond reach. But here's the truth: no one is beyond God's light. Not Saul. Not Foster. Not you.

Reflection Questions:

What areas of your life need a Damascus moment?

How has God already begun to shift your direction?

Who in your life needs to hear that change is possible through Jesus?

Challenge:

Take 15 minutes today to journal or pray about one part of your life where you need transformation. Ask God for a clear next step—and the courage to take it.

One encounter with Jesus can change your story forever.

Day 17: Faith in the Lions' Den

Scripture:

Daniel 6:22–23 (ESV)

"My God sent his angel and shut the lions' mouths, and they have not harmed me... Then the king was exceedingly glad... and no kind of harm was found on him, because he had trusted in his God."

Devotion:

Daniel didn't fight the lions—he trusted the One who could. Surrounded by teeth and shadows, he wasn't spared from the den—but he was protected through it. Because faith doesn't guarantee avoidance. It guarantees presence.

In *Finding God in the Mountains of Afghanistan*, there were moments when Stache's squad felt like they were sitting in the den—ambushed, overwhelmed, encircled by threats they couldn't see coming. But what held them steady wasn't firepower. It was faith.

You may not be facing literal lions, but your own "den" might be loneliness, addiction, fear, or doubt. Know this: God still sends angels. He still shuts mouths. He still honors those who trust Him.

Reflection Questions:

What does your lions' den look like right now?

How has God shown up for you in dark, uncertain places?

What would it look like to trust Him more fully—right where you are?

Challenge:

Take a moment today to write or speak this out: "God, I trust You in the den." Let that be your declaration, no matter how loud the lions seem.

Faith doesn't fear the den—it invites God into it.

Day 18: Victory from Setback

Scripture:

Joshua 8:1 (ESV)

"And the Lord said to Joshua, 'Do not fear and do not be dismayed. Take all the fighting men with you... I have given into your hand the king of Ai, and his people, his city, and his land.'"

Devotion:

After a painful defeat, God told Joshua to try again. But this time, He went with them.

In *Finding God in the Mountains of Afghanistan*, not every mission went as planned. Mistakes were made. People got hurt. But God never let failure have the final word. He brought wisdom through every loss.

Failure doesn't disqualify you—it refocuses you. And when God says go again, it means the outcome is already in His hands.

Reflection Questions:

What past failure is still shaping your mindset?

Where might God be inviting you to try again—with Him?

How can your setbacks prepare you for spiritual success?

Challenge:

Write down a past setback and pray over it. Ask God how He wants to use it in your next victory.

Your last battle doesn't define you. God's promise does.

Day 19: The Prayer that Changed Everything

Scripture:

1 Chronicles 4:10 (ESV)

"Jabez called upon the God of Israel... 'Oh that you would bless me and enlarge my border...' And God granted what he asked."

Devotion:

Jabez's story is brief—but his prayer is bold. He asked for blessing, expansion, protection, and peace. And God answered.

In *Finding God in the Mountains of Afghanistan*, some of the most powerful moments came not from combat, but from quiet prayers. When men asked God to move—not just on the mission, but in their hearts—He did.

Your prayer life is your front line. Pray like it matters. Because it does.

Reflection Questions:

What would it look like to pray boldly today?

Are you asking God for just enough—or for more than enough?

How can you begin each day with a prayer like Jabez?

Challenge:

Write your own version of the Prayer of Jabez. Personalize it—and declare it over your life.

God honors bold prayers because bold prayers honor God.

Day 20: Coming Home

Scripture:

Luke 15:20–24 (ESV)

"But while he was still a long way off, his father saw him... ran and embraced him... 'For this my son was dead, and is alive again; he was lost, and is found.'"

Devotion:

The prodigal didn't come home with a speech—he came home with repentance. And the Father ran to meet him.

In *Finding God in the Mountains of Afghanistan*, the journey home wasn't just about landing in the States. It was about being spiritually found—learning that God doesn't greet you with shame, but with celebration.

No matter how far you've run or how long you've been away, your Father is still looking for you. He hasn't moved. Come home.

Reflection Questions:

What's been keeping you from running back to God?

How does the Father's embrace change your view of repentance?

Who in your life needs to hear that home is still possible?

Challenge:

Find a quiet space. Read Luke 15 slowly. Picture the Father running toward you—and let that truth sink deep.

Grace doesn't wait on the porch. It runs.

Day 21: More Than Enough

Scripture:

John 6:10–11 (ESV)

"Jesus then took the loaves... and distributed them... So also the fish, as much as they wanted."

Devotion:

Five loaves. Two fish. Thousands fed. But the miracle wasn't just in the math—it was in the moment of surrender.

In *Finding God in the Mountains of Afghanistan*, provision didn't always come from warehouses. Sometimes it came through unexpected kindness, shared supplies, or favor at the exact moment it was needed.

God still multiplies. What you think is small can become more than enough in His hands.

Reflection Questions:

What's one area in your life where you feel lack?

How can you offer what you have to God, no matter how small?

What "loaves and fish" moment can you look back on with gratitude?

Challenge:

Give something today—time, energy, a resource. Watch how God uses it to bless others.

God doesn't need more—He just needs what you've got.

Day 22: Praising Through the Prison

Scripture:

Acts 16:25–26 (ESV)

"About midnight Paul and Silas were praying and singing hymns to God… and suddenly there was a great earthquake… all the doors were opened, and everyone's bonds were unfastened."

Devotion:

They weren't praising because they were free—they praised while still bound.

In *Finding God in the Mountains of Afghanistan*, worship didn't wait for ideal conditions. It happened in tents, in chow halls, and even in silence. Praise was their protest against despair.

Your "prison" might be emotional, spiritual, or situational. But chains break when hearts lift.

Reflection Questions:

What prison are you in right now?

What would it look like to praise God before the breakthrough?

How can your worship influence others around you?

Challenge:

Play a worship song today—even if you don't feel like it. Sing, listen, or just let the words fill your space.

Sometimes praise is your most powerful weapon.

Day 23: Courage in Your Calling

Scripture:

Esther 4:14 (ESV)

"And who knows whether you have not come to the kingdom for such a time as this?"

Devotion:

Esther didn't ask for the spotlight—but she stepped into it. Her people were at risk, and God had placed her in a position to speak up. It wasn't easy. It wasn't safe. But it was necessary.

In *Finding God in the Mountains of Afghanistan*, courage didn't always look like action—it sometimes looked like obedience. There were moments when someone had to speak up, step in, or stand alone. Like Esther, they didn't feel ready. But they were called.

You may not be in a palace, but you are in a position. And God may be calling you to something bigger than your comfort zone.

Reflection Questions:

Where is God asking you to act with courage today?

What fears or excuses do you need to surrender?

How can your obedience impact others around you?

Challenge:

Identify one area where you've been silent out of fear. Ask God for the boldness to step forward—"for such a time as this."

You don't need to feel ready—you just need to be willing.

Day 24: Faith Under Command

Scripture:

Matthew 8:8–10 (ESV)

"But the centurion replied, 'Lord, I am not worthy... but only say the word, and my servant will be healed...' When Jesus heard this, he marveled... 'With no one in Israel have I found such faith.'"

Devotion:

The centurion understood authority—and faith. He didn't need Jesus to follow him home. He just needed Jesus to speak.

In *Finding God in the Mountains of Afghanistan*, soldiers like Stache learned to trust the unseen chain of command—both on earth and in heaven. They knew that orders carried weight, and so does the Word of God.

Sometimes the strongest faith isn't loud. It's humble. It says, "Just speak, Lord, and I'll believe."

Reflection Questions:

Where do you need to trust God's word more than your own understanding?

How does the centurion's humility challenge your view of authority and trust?

How can you submit your life to God's command today?

Challenge:

Pick a specific promise from Scripture. Speak it over your life like a standing order—and walk in that truth today.

Faith doesn't always move mountains. Sometimes it just moves us to trust.

Day 25: Called from the Start

Scripture:

Jeremiah 1:5–8 (ESV)

"Before I formed you in the womb I knew you... Do not be afraid... for I am with you to deliver you, declares the Lord."

Devotion:

Jeremiah didn't feel qualified. Too young. Too unsure. Too human. But God wasn't asking for experience—He was asking for obedience.

In *Finding God in the Mountains of Afghanistan*, many young soldiers wrestled with purpose and fear. But calling isn't about comfort—it's about the God who called you long before you stepped into the fight.

You are not accidental. You were chosen on purpose, for a purpose.

Reflection Questions:

What lies have you believed about your worth or ability?

How does knowing God called you before you were born change your perspective?

Who can you affirm in their calling today?

Challenge:

Write a note to yourself—or someone else—reminding them that God knew and chose them before they were ever ready.

You were called before you were capable—and that's the point.

Day 26: Leadership Starts at the Feet

Scripture:

John 13:14–15 (ESV)

"If I then, your Lord and Teacher, have washed your feet, you also ought to wash one another's feet... I have given you an example."

Devotion:

Jesus had nothing to prove. And yet He knelt.

True leadership isn't about rank—it's about responsibility. Jesus showed that the highest calling is often found at the lowest place.

In *Finding God in the Mountains of Afghanistan*, some of the strongest leaders weren't the loudest. They were the ones who served first, asked last, and made sure others ate before they did.

Want to lead like Jesus? Grab a towel.

Reflection Questions:

How does Jesus' servant leadership model challenge your view of influence?

What does it look like to wash feet in your current context?

How can you lead someone this week through humility and love?

Challenge:

Find one practical way to serve someone today—without expecting anything in return.

You don't need a title to lead—just a towel.

Day 27: A Glimpse of Glory

Scripture:

Matthew 17:2–5 (ESV)

"And he was transfigured before them... a voice from the cloud said, 'This is my beloved Son... listen to him.'"

Devotion:

The mountaintop didn't last—but the moment changed everything.

Peter, James, and John saw Jesus in His glory, and it left them in awe. Sometimes God gives us glimpses—not to keep us there, but to strengthen us for the valley.

In *Finding God in the Mountains of Afghanistan*, moments of worship, peace, or unexpected beauty reminded the soldiers they were not forgotten. These mountaintop moments didn't last—but they were enough.

Sometimes all we need is a glimpse to keep going.

Reflection Questions:

When has God given you a glimpse of His glory or presence?

How do those moments shape how you trust Him in harder seasons?

Who do you need to remind today that He is still present?

Challenge:

Reflect on a moment where you sensed God's presence deeply. Write it down. Thank Him—and carry it into the valley.

Glimpses of glory are anchors for the storms ahead.

Day 28: Reluctant Obedience, Radical Grace

Scripture:

Jonah 3:4–5 (ESV)

"Jonah began to go into the city, going a day's journey. And he called out, 'Yet forty days, and Nineveh shall be overthrown!' And the people of Nineveh believed God…"

Devotion:

Jonah ran. Then obeyed. Then pouted. And still— God moved. Not because Jonah was perfect, but because God is gracious.

In *Finding God in the Mountains of Afghanistan*, obedience wasn't always enthusiastic. Sometimes it came after hesitation, frustration, or fatigue. But when obedience came, God worked through it.

Maybe you don't feel ready. Maybe you're frustrated. But God still wants to use your voice. Even reluctant obedience can lead to radical redemption.

Reflection Questions:

Where have you been resisting God's call?

What does obedience look like—even when it's reluctant?

Who might be waiting on your faithfulness to hear about God's mercy?

Challenge:

Write down what God has asked you to do—and one step you can take toward obeying it today.

Even reluctant obedience can release revival.

Day 29: Not My Will

Scripture:

Matthew 26:39 (ESV)

"And going a little farther he fell on his face and prayed, saying, 'My Father, if it be possible, let this cup pass from me; nevertheless, not as I will, but as you will.'"

Devotion:

Jesus didn't just pray in Gethsemane—He surrendered. Even when it hurt. Especially when it hurt.

In *Finding God in the Mountains of Afghanistan*, surrender wasn't just about tactics. It was about hearts. About letting go of the illusion of control and trusting God's plan over personal preference.

You may be facing something hard today. A decision. A diagnosis. A delay. But real strength comes when we lay it all down and say, "Your will, not mine."

Reflection Questions:

What situation in your life are you trying to control?

How does Jesus' surrender challenge your response to hardship?

What would it mean to truly pray, "Not my will, but Yours" today?

Challenge:

Pray a full-surrender prayer today. Name what you're holding onto—and release it into God's hands.

Surrender isn't weakness. It's where strength begins.

Day 30: Your Mission Continues

Scripture:

Matthew 28:18–20 (ESV)

"And Jesus came and said to them, 'All authority... has been given to me. Go therefore and make disciples... and behold, I am with you always, to the end of the age.'"

Devotion:

Jesus didn't just rescue you—He deployed you.

The Great Commission isn't just a command—it's a calling. A lifelong mission to bring hope, truth, and grace to every corner of the world. That includes your home. Your squad. Your workplace. Your social circles.

In *Finding God in the Mountains of Afghanistan*, the mission didn't end with a flight home. It continued—in faith, in purpose, and in the calling to carry God's love forward.

You've spent 30 days drawing closer to God. Now go live it out. The mission field is everywhere your boots land.

Reflection Questions:

Where is God calling you to carry His message next?

Who around you needs the hope you now hold?

What will "going" look like for you starting today?

Challenge:

Reach out to someone today who needs encouragement. Share one thing God taught you during this challenge—and invite them to walk with you.

The mission isn't over. It's just beginning.

About the Author

Joshua Pennifield is a U.S. Army Staff Sergeant and a graduate of Liberty University, where he earned his degree in Data Networking and Security. He is a combat-tested leader and a follower of Christ who has found purpose through both military service and a personal walk of faith.

Joshua's writing is born out of real experience—on dusty roads, in moments of doubt, and through everyday challenges where God showed up with power and grace. His hope is to reach fellow service members, veterans, and anyone navigating their own spiritual battles.

He lives in Virginia with his wife, Rachel, and is passionate about helping others find peace, purpose, and identity through Christ in every season of life.